Where The Hell Had His Boys Found Her?

"Boys!" he shouted as he bunched the thick white terry cloth around his waist.

They were far too clever to answer.

She turned off the faucets and said quietly, "It's not their fault, you know."

"Don't defend them. Who the hell are you anyway?" Lucas whispered, too hotly aware of her lithe golden body to be able to speak. "How long have you been living—"

But he already knew. "Eleven days?" he croaked.

Her face turned crimson. She nodded.

She was the pet. She was the mysterious angelic presence he'd sensed in the house who'd magically improved his life with his sons. Her spell was so powerful she'd even managed to insert herself into his dreams.

No wonder his boys had been determined to fire all those nannies and stay home and tend her....

Dear Reader,

It's hard to believe that this is the grand finale of CELEBRATION 1000! But all good things must come to an end. Not that there aren't more wonderful things in store for you next month, too....

But as for June, first we have an absolutely sizzling MAN OF THE MONTH from Ann Major called *The Accidental Bodyguard.*

Are you a fan of HAWK'S WAY? If so, don't miss the latest "Hawk's" story, *The Temporary Groom* by Joan Johnston. Check out the family tree on page six and see if you recognize all the members of the Whitelaw family.

And with *The Cowboy and the Cradle* Cait London has begun a fabulous new western series—THE TALLCHIEFS. (P.S. The next Tallchief is all set for September!)

Many of you have written to say how much you love Elizabeth Bevarly's books. Her latest, *Father of the Brood,* book #2 in the FROM HERE TO PATERNITY series, simply shouldn't be missed.

This month is completed with Karen Leabo's *The Prodigal Groom,* the latest in our WEDDING NIGHT series, and don't miss a wonderful star of tomorrow— DEBUT AUTHOR Eileen Wilks, who's written *The Loner and the Lady.*

As for next month...we have a not-to-be-missed MAN OF THE MONTH by Anne McAllister, and Dixie Browning launches DADDY KNOWS LAST, a new Silhouette continuity series beginning in Desire.

Lucia Macro

Senior Editor

Please address questions and book requests to:
Silhouette Reader Service
U.S.: 3010 Walden Ave., P.O. Box 1325, Buffalo, NY 14269
Canadian: P.O. Box 609, Fort Erie, Ont. L2A 5X3

Ann Major

THE ACCIDENTAL BODYGUARD

SILHOUETTE *Desire*®
Published by Silhouette Books
America's Publisher of Contemporary Romance

SILHOUETTE BOOKS

ISBN 0-373-76003-5

THE ACCIDENTAL BODYGUARD

Books by Ann Major

ANN MAJOR

loves writing romance novels as much as she loves reading them. She is the proud mother of three children who are now in high school and college. She lists hiking in the Colorado mountains with her husband, playing tennis, sailing, enjoying her cats and playing the piano among her favorite activities.

Dear Reader,

I am very thrilled to be part of the CELEBRATION 1000 for the Silhouette Desire line, and I hope each of you will enjoy *The Accidental Bodyguard*.

My books always seem to me to be like patchwork quilts. I mix my experiences and reactions with the stories other people tell me and the things I read, and out comes a story. Not that this is an easy process. Not that when I am done I can't still remember the agony of every bad idea and every ripped-out seam.

My husband is a doctor, and I had originally intended to write a story about the skeleton of an Indian girl that hangs in his office. I remember when a great big crate from India arrived—years ago—and we went up after work with the children and pried the lid off the carton. We found a beautiful, carefully packed skeleton inside. My husband said she couldn't have been older than eighteen when she died. We were all deeply awed as he gently lifted the skeleton out and we all wondered who she had been and how she had lived.

This book began with my questions about that girl, and I thought I would be writing about a skeleton coming to life and changing a doctor's life. But as I began to research the story and read about reincarnation, I began wondering about other mysteries.

Why do we sometimes feel we know a person instantly? Why do new patterns and new places sometimes feel so familiar? Why do some souls seem so much wiser than others? How can a person fall in love instantly? As you will see, there is no skeleton in my story. When I sat down to write, my imagination twisted and turned and I wrote an entirely different book than the one I had envisioned.

But what stayed the same was my great curiosity about life and death and the boundaries of love.

Enjoy.

Ann Major

Prologue

"Chandra is a conniving little do-goody bitch!" Holly said.

The rest of the family, which included, among others, Holly's parents, Ned and Sandra Moran, as well as her husband, Stinky Brown, and his brother, Hal, nodded in silent unison.

Lucas Broderick stopped scribbling on his legal pad and lifted his head to observe the young woman who spoke so vehemently against the cousin who was to gain control of the Moran fortune.

Holly Moran had chocolate-dark curls, an hour-glass figure and a flare for drama a trial lawyer such as Lucas couldn't help but envy. She still had on the black sheath and the rope of pearls she had worn to her grandmother's funeral. But the dark eyes that locked with Lucas's were clear and lovely, unmarred by any trace of grief as she let him know that even though she was married, she was hot and...available.

A billion dollars was one hell of a turn-on. Well, almost a billion, give or take a hundred million or two.

Holly was as drop-dead gorgeous and just as drop-dead mean as his ex-wife, Joan, had been. Holly had that too-bright glow of a woman who hadn't yet settled comfortably into marriage. For half a second, Lucas, who was lonely for the kind of pleasure a woman like Holly could provide, was tempted.

Then his rational mind clicked in.

Been there. Done that.

His steel-gray eyes glittered as he gave her an ironic smile. *Been taken in by that act before, pretty lady.*

The last thing he needed was another Joan. His ex-wife had given him the shaft and taken him to the cleaners as nobody had since he'd been a green kid. As no woman ever would again.

He'd given his heart to Joan, and she'd ripped it out while it was still beating. She had taken most of his money, and she'd done a number on their sons.

His enemies said he had no heart. Who needed one?

Holly's silky voice grew more vicious, not that she was addressing anybody in particular. "I tell you her do-goody act was all fake. How could Gram have left everything to her?"

"Not quite everything," Uncle Henry dared to object. "Gertie did leave each of us two—"

Of the four voices that shouted him down, Holly's was the softest, and the angriest.

"She might as well have! You may be able to get by on a lousy million or two since you're content to live in that miserable unair-conditioned shack on your godforsaken farm like a hermit.''

For three hours the Morans had been ranting about Gertrude Moran's will in the ranch house's richly paneled library while Lucas, their legal hired gun, had reposed in a deep leather armchair, listening impassively as he watched the clouds move in and thicken against the distant horizon. Occasionally he wrote down a note or two on his yellow pad, which he would probably never so much as glance at again.

Much had been written about the rugged, legendary lawyer who was now sprawled in the library's most comfortable chair in scuffed boots, faded jeans and a crisp white shirt. But the majority of the press coverage was false.

Lucas could have told the Morans a thing or two about poverty, more than they wanted to know, more than he wanted to remember. For he had been born in India to an impoverished missionary. His father, a zealot and an idealist, had forced his family to live in the same dangerous, squalid slums as the people he helped. Then the old man had given all his love and attention to the impoverished Indians.

Left alone to fend for himself in dangerous neighborhoods, Lucas had been beaten by jeering gangs of bullies more times than he could count, his meager possessions stolen, his emerging male self-confidence shattered. His father's response had been to feel sorry for the young criminals and to tell Lucas to turn the other cheek. Lucas had sworn that when he grew up he would be the fighter and the taker. He would hit hard. Others could turn the other cheek.

But Lucas's real roots were something he worked very hard to conceal. He didn't want anybody to know that he harbored a deep-rooted feeling of abandonment and poor self-esteem. He wanted people to think he was tough and cruel—a winner. So he manipulated his public image as ruthlessly as he manipulated the minds of jurors when he made them believe the most preposterous arguments, or as easily as he convinced clients like the Morans they couldn't possibly get what they wanted without him. His profession was a high-stakes game, which he always played to win.

Texas journalists loved to quote him. "God may have created the world, but the Devil put the spin on it." "Ten thousand times more crimes have been committed in the name of love than in the name of hate." "No good deed goes unpunished." These cynical if less than original statements, which seemed to sum up his philosophy about life, had appeared in dozens of profiles of him in Texas magazines and newspapers.

He was widely hated and only grudgingly admired. Flamboyant quotes were hardly Lucas's only talent. He was a superb athlete, and he excelled in mathematics. He automatically converted everything into numbers—especially his time, that being to him the most valuable of all commodities because, once it was gone, it was gone forever.

Since all Lucas's clients bombarded him with tales of woe, he usually found these long preliminary consultations tiresome, especially if he was expected to fake compassion. But the Morans' tale was too bizarre and their threatened fortune too huge for their story not to compel his full attention. He was struggling to pretend sympathy. What the hell? He'd sold himself before for a lot less than a billion.

While Holly attacked Stinky for always taking Beth's side and not seeing her as a threat before today, Lucas reviewed his notes.

The family's do-goody dark horse, a Miss Bethany Ann—he'd made a scribble that she wanted to be called Chandra—had come from out of nowhere and galloped away with the family fortune.

Both the girl and her story intrigued him. He furrowed his black brows as he tried to read his nearly illegible scrawl.

Bulk of fortune goes into charitable foundation. Complete control given to Miss Bethany Ann.

Weird little girl. Prematurely born in Calcutta when her mother and father were on a round-the-world tour.

India—so he and she had been born in the same hellhole.

An oddball from birth, she was claustrophobic. She was also a vegetarian who refused to eat beef. Never fit into the family. When she was two and had begun to talk, she'd told her family that her name was Chandra, not Beth. She had babbled frantically of memories of another life and of belonging to another, poorer family. When she grew older she said her enraged older sister, in an effort to save the family from shame, had shut her inside a box and buried her alive beneath a house when she found out Chandra had gotten pregnant by the town's local bad boy whom she loved instead of her betrothed.

Under hypnosis Chandra had spoken in a foreign language that a language expert at the University of Texas had identified as an obscure dialect of Hindi.

Upon investigation, a family in a remote area of India where this dialect was spoken had been found. Names, dates and facts of this family's history exactly fit Chandra's story.

Gertrude and all the Morans had flown to India. A seven-year-old Chandra had led everybody to a ruined house and insisted they dig up a brick floor. Chandra's former sister, a woman by then in her mid-fifties, had burst into guilty tears when a crumbling box with the bones of a young girl and those of her unborn child had been discovered, and Chandra had accused her of burying her alive. The grave of the dead girl's bad-boy lover was visited next. Apparently he had stepped in front of a train and had been sliced to death shortly after he'd been told that the dead girl had run away.

Weird. Lucas, who knew more than he wanted to about India and reincarnation, had underlined the word three times. This girl, Bethany, Chandra, whatever, had wanted to share the Moran money with those less fortunate. Understandably alarmed, the entire Moran clan had been determined to erase the inappropriate "memories" and eradicate such inappropriate attitudes. They had taken the little girl to countless doctors, psychologists, and finally to a hypnotist who was no help at all, since he had said this looked like a genuine case of reincarnation if ever there was one. He pointed out that Chandra's claustrophobia was perfectly natural under such circumstances.

Gertrude Moran had fired the hypnotist on the spot and refused to take the child to any more "charlatans." After Bethany's parents had been killed in a car accident, the old lady had done everything in her power to make the girl forget her "former life" and mold her into a true Moran. But the impossible child had been kicked out of every fancy boarding school she'd been sent to, and the old lady had had to take charge of the girl's education herself. Gertrude had taken the child everywhere and taught her about investments, real estate, bonds, ranching and stocks.

But apparently the shape of Bethany's personality had been as difficult as the old lady's. Not that the girl hadn't appeared gentle and loving and generous and biddable. But no matter how intelligent and receptive she had seemed on the surface, her character had been as true to its own shape as the most uncarvable stone. She continued to sympathize with those less fortunate than she. At the age of twelve she had her name legally changed to Chandra. As she grew older she had a tendency to date bad boys—because she said she was looking for the man she had loved in her former life. When she was eighteen and on the brink of marriage to Stinky Brown, a slick charmer Gertrude Moran had considered totally unsuitable, she and her grandmother had had a disastrous quarrel. Chandra had broken off with Stinky and run away without a dime, never to be seen or spoken of or to again.

Until now.

For a fleeting moment Lucas felt an unwanted respect for a girl who could stand up to Gertrude Moran and walk away from such a huge fortune. Then he reminded himself there was no such thing as selfless good, that somebody always paid.

Lucas's last words on the yellow page were Holly's. "The conniving little do-goody bitch. I tell you her do-goody act was all fake."

Could be, pretty lady. Fortune hunters and con artists damn sure came in all sorts of interesting shapes and varieties. But this kid with the innocent face and the freckles and the masses of golden hair was damn good.

Lucas lifted a picture of a seven-year-old girl standing before a hut in India with her "other family." Next he looked at a grainy black-and-white newspaper picture of her standing beside some look-alike heiress buddy named Cathy Calderon. They both wore ragged jeans, steel-toed work boots and hard hats as they posed in front of a concrete blockhouse one of her church groups had recently completed for a Mexican family.

Couldn't tell much other than the fact that Bethany Chandra damn sure had long legs and a cute butt.

Been there. Long legs and a cute butt had cost him big time. Joan had *started* by taking half of his estate. She'd won child support, lots of it. Then she'd dumped the boys back on him.

His housekeeper had quit the first day, shaking both fists and screaming, "Your sons are savages, Mr. Broderick. If you don't pack them off to a military school, and soon, you'll be sorry."

No housekeeper he'd hired since had lasted more than a week, and his once elegant house was a shambles.

Forget Joan and the housekeeper problem.

The intriguing fortune hunter with the intriguing backside was living in an impoverished barrio and running a huge, privately endowed, highly successful, nonprofit organization called Casas de Cristo, which built houses for the poor all over northern Mexico. She had tribes of wealthy philanthropists who trusted her enough to donate their millions. She had church groups and college kids from all over the United States providing money and free labor.

Missionaries were a tiresome, impractical breed. He should know. His father had played at saving the world. What the hell? The more starving Indians he'd fed, the more babies they'd produced with more mouths to be fed. One thing was sure. The old man had damn sure failed to provide for his own sons. Lucas had had to work his tail off to get a start at the good life.

Thus, Lucas was mildly surprised that he felt such distaste at the thought of defaming this girl when such an immense fortune and therefore his own lucrative fee were at stake. All he had to do was drum up a few witnesses to say that Bethany was cheating her benefactors by building her houses for less than she said or that she was taking bribes from the poor families selected to have houses built for them.

He loathed do-gooders. Why should it bother him that there wasn't a shred of evidence that she was anything other than what she appeared to be—that rare and highly bizarre individual like his father who actually wanted to help other people?

Odd that he didn't particularly relish having to prove that Gertrude Moran had been senile when she'd drawn up her new will, either.

But that last part would be easier.

A flash of movement flickered across the golden urn that sat in the center of a library table. The urn, conspicuously located but now forgotten, was surrounded by stacks of legal documents, coffee cups, wineglasses, beer bottles and half-eaten sandwiches. Lucas glanced from it out the window, where he got a double surprise.

The sky was now an eerie green. A dark man in a black Stetson sat in a blue van parked beside his Lincoln. After studying the storm clouds and the newcomer for a tense moment, Lucas relaxed, dismissing them both as of no immediate importance.

Not that the Morans had noticed either the clouds or the van. And they had quit all pretense of interest in the urn that contained Gertrude Moran's ashes immediately after the reading of her will, at which point they'd started hunting their lawyer.

Fortunately Lucas had been close by in San Antonio visiting Pete, his older brother, who was a doctor.

Lucas leaned forward in his chair and lifted the urn with his left hand. Whatever he had seen there had vanished. All he saw now was his own brooding dark face and his thick tumble of unruly black hair. Turning the urn carelessly with his other hand, he glanced at the portrait of the woman whose ashes he held.

Gertrude Moran's sharp, painted eyes glinted at him with an expression of don't-you-dare-try-to-mess-with-me-you-young-upstart. In old age with her soft snowy hair, she had remained a handsome woman. Holly had told Lucas that the portrait had been finished less than a month ago. Lucas found it hard to imagine someone who looked so forceful and intelligent not knowing exactly what she was doing when she'd drawn up her will.

Gertrude Moran had been shrewd all her life. The original Moran fortune had been in land and oil. She'd diversified, doubling her fortune while other oil people went broke. In an age when most rich people were stuffy and dull, she had been a hoot. The newspapers had been full of her stunts.

Lucas lowered his gaze. Well, she'd damn sure stirred the family brew by secretly changing all the ingredients in her will and leaving only a few million to these spoiled bastards.

"Well, Mr. Broderick, can you get us our money back or not?" Holly leaned forward and issued another invitation with her dark, glowing eyes and a display of cleavage.

Been there, he reminded himself, but he dropped the urn with a clang.

Stinky jumped as if he was afraid Gertrude's spirit would spring out of the urn like a bad genie. A hush fell over the room, and for a long moment it did seem, even to Lucas, that those keen, painted eyes brightened with mischief and that some bold, alien presence had invaded the room.

He almost felt like clanging the urn again to break the spell.

His hard face tensed. "Can I get the money?" He leafed through the will. "It's a crapshoot. It's not too difficult to break a will that involves leaving one family member an entire fortune at the expense of the others. But charitable foundations with iron-clad, carefully thought out legal documents such as these are tricky, especially when the foundation will con-

tribute substantially to several powerhouse charities
who have teams of lawyers on their payroll."

"But Beth bamboozled Gram into giving her everything—"

"Not quite everything. Your grandmother did ade-
quately provide for you. At least most judges would
see it that way. Technically your cousin won't actually be inheriting the fortune, Ms. Moran. She would
merely be managing the foundation."

"For a huge salary?"

"A six-figure annual salary for overseeing such a
vast enterprise would hardly be out of line."

"Beth is a thief and a criminal."

Lucas felt an insane urge to defend the absent heiress.

"Those are serious charges that might not be so
easily proven. From the picture you've drawn of
Beth—a goody-two-shoes Samaritan building houses
for the poor in Mexico—it might be difficult and unpleasant to convince twelve disinterested people she
wouldn't sincerely honor your grandmother's last
wishes. If she's a fake, we've got a chance. But if she's
not—" He paused. "Unfortunately juries and judges
have a tendency to favor do-gooders. I suggest that
you talk to your cousin. Try to persuade her it would
be in her best interests to divide the money between all
of you."

"You have no idea how stubborn she is."

"Maybe one of you will come up with a better
idea."

A pair of black-lashed, olive-bright eyes set in a
gorgeous face met his, and Lucas was chilled when he
sensed a terrible hatred and an implacable will.

The black clouds were rolling in from the west. The mood in the library had darkened, as well. Other faces turned toward him, and they were equally hard.

Lucas almost shuddered. No wonder the saint had run.

Strangely, his feelings of empathy for the girl intensified. He tried to fight the softening inside him, but it was almost as though he was on her side instead of the Morans'.

Ridiculous. He couldn't afford such misplaced sympathies.

"If you take the case, how much will you charge?" Holly demanded.

"If I lose—nothing."

"And—if you win?"

"I would be working on a contingency basis, of course—"

"How much?"

"Forty percent. Plus expenses."

"Of nearly a billion dollars! What? Are you mad? Why, that's highway robbery."

"No, Ms. Moran, it's my fee. I play for keeps—all or nothing. If you want me, and if I agree to take the case, I swear to you that if there is any way to destroy your cousin's name and her claim to your fortune, I'll find it. I am very thorough and utterly merciless when it comes to matters of this nature. I'll study these documents and send my P.I. to Mexico to investigate Casas de Cristo and see what dirt I can dig up on her down there. She's bound to have enemies. All we have to do is find people who'll talk about her and get them talking. Fan the flames, so to speak."

Lucas began gathering documents and stuffing them into his briefcase. "Just so you can reach me any-time—" He scribbled his unlisted home phone number and handed it to Stinky. "I'll let myself out."

Lightning streaked to the ground. Almost immediately a sharp cracking sound shook the house. Wind and torrents of rain began to batter the windows.

The drought was over.

But none of the ranchers who had prayed for rain rejoiced. They were watching Lucas's large brown hands violently snap the locks on his briefcase as he prepared to go.

The mood in the library had grown as ugly and dangerous as the storm outside. The Morans were in that no-win situation so many people involved in litigation find themselves. They were wondering whom they disliked the most—their adversary, the family saint, or their own utterly ruthless but highly reputed attorney.

One minute Lucas was bursting out of the library doors into the foyer, intent on nothing except driving to San Antonio as fast as possible. In the next minute, Lucas felt as if he'd been sucked blindly into a cyclone and hurled into an entirely new reality in which an incredibly powerful force gripped him, body and soul. In which all his dark bitternesses miraculously dissolved. Even his fierce ambition to work solely for money was gone.

Unsuperstitious by nature, Lucas did not believe in psychic powers or ghosts. But this otherworldly experience was a very pleasurable feeling.

Dangerously pleasurable. Almost sexual, and dangerously familiar somehow.

All his life he'd been driven by anger and greed or by the quest for power.

And suddenly those drives were gone. What he really wanted was in this room.

He stopped in midstride. His huge body whirled; his searing gray eyes searched every niche and darkened corner of the hall.

The mysterious presence was very near. As he stood there, he continued to feel the weird, overpowering connection.

She was as afraid of this thing as he was.

She?

For no reason at all Lucas was reminded of the times he and his brother, Pete, had hidden together as children from the Indian slum bullies, not speaking to one another but each profoundly aware of the other.

"Hello?" Lucas's deep querying drawl held a baffled note.

He held his breath. For the first time he noted how eerily quiet the foyer was. How the presence of death seemed to linger like an unwanted guest.

How the hall with its pale green wallpaper was heavy with the odor of roses past their prime. How these swollen blossoms, no doubt leftovers from Gertrude Moran's memorial service, were massed everywhere—in vases, in Meissen bowls. How several white petals had fallen onto the polished tabletops and floors. Holly had shown him the old lady's rose garden and had told him she had loved roses.

Lucas's senses were strangely heightened as he stood frozen outside the library doors, struggling to figure out what was happening to him. He inhaled the sickly-sweet, funereal scent of the dying roses. He listened to each insistent tick of the vermeil clock.

The summer sunlight was fading. Much of the white and gilt furniture was cast in shadow. The threadbare Aubusson rug at his feet had a forest green border.

When he saw the closet with its door standing partially ajar, he felt strangely drawn to it. Oddly enough, when he stepped toward it, the connection was instantly broken. He was free.

All his old bitterness and cynicism immediately regained him.

He bolted out of the Moran mansion faster than before.

One

"Kill!"

Sweet P.'s earsplitting voice blasted inside Lucas's black Lincoln as he raced toward the hospital. The shrieks seemed to slice open his skull and shred the tender tissues of his inner ear as handily as a meat cleaver.

There should be a law against a three-year-old screaming in an automobile speeding sixty miles per hour on a freeway.

Just as there should be a law against a kid being up at five in the morning experimenting with her older cousin's handcuffs.

Just as there should be a law against Peppin owning a pair of the damn things in the first place.

"You get off here," Pete suddenly said as they were about to pass the exit ramp.

Tires screamed as Lucas swerved across two lanes onto the down ramp.

"Mommy! Carol!" Patti yelled between sobs.

Too bad Mommy was out of town and Carol, her sitter, had called in sick.

Patti shook her hands violently, rattling the handcuffs.

Lucas's temples thudded with equal violence.

It was Monday morning. Six o'clock to be exact. Lucas felt like hell. Usually he never dreamed, but last night a weird nightmare about a girl in trouble had kept him up most of the night. In the dream, he had loved the girl, and they'd been happy for a while. Then she'd been abducted, and he'd found himself alone in a misty landscape of death and stillness and ruin. At first he'd been terrified she was dead. Then she'd made a low moan, and he had known that if he didn't save her, he would lose everything that mattered to him in the world. He'd tracked her through a maze of ruined slums only to find her and have her utter a final low-throated cry and die as he lifted her into his arms. He'd bolted out of his bed, his body drenched in sweat, his heart racing, his sense of tragic loss so overwhelmingly profound he couldn't sleep again.

The girl's ethereally lovely face and voluptuous body had seemed branded into his soul. He'd gotten up and tried to sketch her on his legal notepad. Sleek and slim, she had that classy, rich-girl look magazine editors pay so dearly for. She had high cheekbones, a careless smile, yellow hair and sparkling blue eyes. He'd torn the sheet from the pad and thrown it away, only to sketch another.

Due in court at ten, Lucas had intended to be half-way to Corpus Christi by now. Instead Pete, Sweet P., the boys and he were rushing to the emergency room, where Pete was on call. Some girl had overdosed, and a doctor was needed STAT, medical jargon for fast. Gus, an emergency-room security guard, had volunteered to remove the handcuffs if Pete brought Sweet P. when he came.

Disaster had struck right after Lucas had loaded the luggage and boys into the Lincoln and Pete and Sweet P. had gotten into Pete's Porsche. The Porsche wouldn't start because *someone* had left an interior light on all night.

Someone had also removed Lucas's jumper cables from his trunk. And that same mysterious *someone* had also lost the key to Peppin's handcuffs. Thus, Lucas and the boys had to drive Pete and Sweet P. to the ER before they could head for home.

Why was Lucas even surprised? His personal life had been chaos ever since the boys had moved in. For starters, they must have dialed every nine-hundred number in America, because his phone bill had run into the thousands of dollars the first month they'd lived with him.

Lucas put on his right turn signal when he saw the blue neon sign for San Antonio City Memorial and swerved into the covered parking lot for the hospital's emergency room. With a swoosh of tires and a squeal of brakes, Lucas stopped the big car too suddenly, startling Sweet P. into silence. Her watery blue eyes looked addled as she took in the blazing lights of the three ambulances and the squad car.

Lucas's expression was grim as he lowered the automobile windows, cut the motor and gently gathered Sweet P. into his arms so Pete would be free to check his patient.

As he got out of the Lincoln with the squirming toddler, Lucas gave Peppin and Montague a steely glance. "You two be good."

"No problem." Peppin's sassy grin was all braces. Huge mirrored sunglasses hid his mischievous eyes.

As always Montague, who resented authority, pretended to ignore him and kept his nose in a book entitled *Psychic Vampires*.

The emergency room was such a madhouse, Lucas forgot the boys. Apparently there'd been a fight at the jail. Three prisoners lay on stretchers. A man with hairy armpits and a potbelly wearing only gray Jockey shorts with worn-out elastic was standing outside a treatment room screaming drunkenly that doctors made too much money and he was going to get his lawyer if he didn't get treated at once. In another room an obese woman was pointing to her right side, saying she hurt and that her doctor had spent a fortune on tests and that she was deathly allergic to some kind of pink medicine and that her medical records were in Tyler on microfilm if anybody cared about them. Six telephones buzzed constantly. Doctors were dictating orders to exhausted nurses.

In the confusion it took Lucas a while to find Gus. Meanwhile Sweet P. was so fascinated by the drunk and the fat lady, she stopped crying. Enthroned on the counter of the nurses' station, she was having the time of her life. A plump redheaded nurse was feeding her pizza and candy and cola, which she gobbled greedily while Gus rummaged in a toolbox for the correct pair of bolt cutters.

"Now you hold still, little princess," Gus said.

Suddenly Pete's frantic voice erupted from an examining room down the hall.

"She's gone!"

Lucas left Sweet P. with Gus and raced to the examining room, where an IV dangled over an empty gurney with blood-streaked sheets. Bloody footprints drunkenly crisscrossed the white-tiled floor.

"She has little feet," Lucas whispered inanely, lifting a foot when he realized he was standing squarely on top of two toe prints.

Pete yelled, "Nurse!"

A plump nurse in a blue scrub suit, wearing a plastic ID, ambled inside.

"Oh, my God!"

Pete thumbed hurriedly through the missing patient's chart, reading aloud.

"No name. A Jane Doe. Brought in by a truck driver who found her hitchhiking on the highway. Tested positive for a multitude of legal and illegal drugs. Head injury. Stitches put in by plastic surgeon. Contusions on wrists and ankles. Disruptive. Belligerent. Very confused. Amnesia. Possible subdural hematoma. Refused CAT scan because she went insane when we put her face inside the machine. Claustrophobic."

"What does all that mean?" Lucas demanded.

"Not good. She's high as a kite, badly confused."

"Doctor—" The nurse's whisper was anxious. "A while ago someone called about her. Said he was family. Sounded very concerned. Described a girl who could have been this girl. Sammy's new, and I'm afraid she told him we'd admitted a girl matching her description. The caller said he was coming right over. But when Sammy told the patient that a family member was on his way, she became very agitated.''

"Get security on this immediately," Pete ordered. "This young woman is in no condition to be out of bed. Check the entrances. The parking lots. In her condition she couldn't have gone far."

Fire and ice.

Chilled to the bone, burning up at the same time, the barefoot girl shivered convulsively in the parking lot. Her thoughts kept slipping and losing direction like a sailboat in rough waves.

She didn't know who she was.

Or where she was.

Or who wanted to kill her.

When that freckled nurse had asked her her name, terrible images had rolled through her tired brain.

A name? Something as specific as a name?

"Oh, dear God," had been all she could whisper brokenly.

She could remember the van rolling, catching fire. She kept seeing a gray face, its hideous vacant eyes peering at her through plastic.

Pain and terror shuddered through the injured girl.

They knew who she was, and they were coming after her.

Her head throbbed. When she tried to walk, her gait was wide. Her feet felt like they didn't quite touch the ground, and she had the sensation she was about to topple backward.

Crouching low outside the entrance, the girl had tracked blood down the concrete steps because slivers of glass were still embedded in her heels. Her torn, blood-encrusted jeans and hospital gown clung to her perspiring body like a wet shroud.

Vaguely she remembered someone cutting her red T-shirt and her bra off. Patches of yellow hair were glued to her skull. Dark shadows ringed her blue eyes. She kept swallowing against a dry metallic taste in her mouth. She kept pushing at the loose bandage that hid the row of stitches that were yellow with antiseptic. What was left of a heparin lock oozed blood down her arm.

She had to get out of here.

But how? When ambulances and cops were everywhere?

When those two curious boys in the black Lincoln kept jumping up and down and staring restlessly out of the car.

Feeling muddled, she shut her eyes. Her entire life consisted of a few hours and less than half a dozen foggy memories that made no sense. It was as if she was a child again, and there were monsters in the dark.

Only the monsters were real.

She remembered huge headlights blinding her as she'd thrown herself in front of them. She remembered the frightened trucker, lifting her and demanding angrily, "Girlie, what were you trying to do?" Next she remembered the hospital.

The two boys in the Lincoln must've grown bored with leaning out the windows because all of a sudden they slithered into the front seat like a pair of eels. They leaned over the dashboard, fighting for control of the radio, holding the seek button down through several stations until they came to rap music. Gleefully they slapped their right hands together, turned the volume up and settled back to listen.

"Boys! That's way too loud!"

A stout security officer edged between the girl and the Lincoln. The boy with the slicked-back ponytail and the shark-tooth necklace quirked his head out the window again. When his huge mirrored glasses glinted her way, she was afraid he'd spot her.

"Sure, Officer," he said, clumsily faking a respectful attitude as he thumped the dash with his hand in time to the beat.

The officer lingered a minute or two till the volume was low enough. Only then did he stride away. When he had gone the boy leaned out of the car again, hand still thumping the side of the car as he stared fiercely in the direction of her shadowy hiding place. Twelve, thirteen maybe, he had the surly good looks of a wannabe bad-boy.

The fingers stopped thumping. He yanked off his mirrored glasses and wiggled so far out of the car, he nearly fell.

She heard more sirens in the distance as his gray eyes zeroed in on her.

Dear God.

His sulkily smirking lips mouthed, "Hi." He started to wave.

She put a finger to her lips in warning as two more squad cars, sirens blaring, rushed into the lot. A dozen officers with hand-held radios jumped out.

She shrank more deeply into the shadows, her pleading eyes clutching the smiling boy's as a fat cop shuffled over to the Lincoln.

"You been here awhile, kid?"

The sassy smile faded. He gave the cop a sullen nod.

"You seen anything suspicious?"

Sulky silence. Then slowly the black ponytail bobbed. "Yeah." He pointed toward the alley at the opposite end of the parking lot. "I saw . . . a girl with a—a bandage on her head. Way over there."

The cops shouted to the others and they took off in a dead gallop. When they had disappeared, the boys slapped their right hands together.

Then, ever so cautiously, they eased a door open and scuttled toward her. Hovering over her, their dark narrow faces seemed to waver in and out of focus.

They were so alike they could have passed for twins. Not that they were trying to pass. The taller and skinnier of the two had shorter hair, wire-rimmed glasses and pressed jeans. The huskier kid with the ponytail and the gold earring wore rumpled black clothes. A vicious shark tooth dangled from his necklace.

When they leaned down, their hands, shaking, a whirring sound beat inside her ears and made her feel so dizzy and sick, she almost passed out.

She barely felt their hands as they gently circled her. Or heard their frightened whispers.

"We have to help her."

"But she's hurt. Look at all those bruises, and her eyes—"

"And her feet! We should take her into the hospital so Uncle Pete—"

"No!" She grabbed their arms, her broken nails digging into their skin, her huge eyes pleading.

"Can't you see how scared she is?" a young voice croaked hoarsely. "Somebody bad might be after her. We gotta save her."

"What'll Dad do?"

The whirring inside her head got louder. Half-carrying, half-dragging her, they crawled with her to the car and made a bed of lumpy pillows and blankets for her on the floorboard of the back seat. The boys unfolded a blanket and covered her, whispering that if she was quiet they could smuggle her home and hide her in their room until she got well.

The girl lay there, trembling uncontrollably, terrified of the claustrophobic feeling she had because the blanket was over her face.

Only vaguely was she aware of footsteps hurrying, of car doors slamming, of men's voices talking low in the front seat, of a little girl's excited shouting. "See there! Got 'em off!"

"Oh—big deal."

But the girl in the back seat instantly registered a man's beautiful, gravelly drawl. "Peppin, the officer told me you helped them."

There was something so familiar about the sound of his voice. Something so warm. It seemed to resonate in her soul.

She knew him. She had loved him. Somewhere. Some time.

"Yeah, Dad. Peppin really helped 'em," the older boy said.

"Shut up, Monty!" Peppin slugged his brother.

"Hey!"

"Who are all the cops looking for anyway, Dad?"

"Some young girl got high on drugs and had a wreck. It's a very serious situation. She could die without proper medical attention."

The girl felt hot all over. Tears pooled in her eyes.

"Die?" Peppin croaked as a key turned in the ignition. His young face bleached a sickly white, he stared at his tearful hideaway.

She shook her head at him, tears escaping under her eyelids.

Peppin sucked in a long, nervous breath. "So—Uncle Pete, what sort of treatment would she need?"

"Hmm?"

"Your patient?"

Peppin bombarded his uncle with questions, demanding specific details.

Once again Peppin's father praised his son in that deep melodious drawl of his—this time for his intellectual curiosity.

The man's low voice was husky and somehow devastatingly familiar, and yet at the same time it lulled her. She wanted to go on listening to it, for nothing seemed left in the whole world but that voice wrapping around her.

Who was he? Why did she feel she knew him?

She was too tired for thought, and her eyelids grew heavy again, fluttering down and then rising as she fought to stay awake.

She slept soundly for the first time since the van had rolled and the driver had chased her into those blinding headlights.

She slept, knowing she was safe, because the man with the beautiful voice was near.

Two

Bluish flashes ricocheted in the boys' bedroom.

It had rained like this the night the blue van had rolled and burned.

What van? Where? Why?

The girl lay rigidly awake, longing for Lucas as she listened to the surf and to the sharp cracking sounds of thunder. Torrents of rain beat a savage tattoo against the bedroom window.

He was two doors down from her. Peacefully asleep in his huge bed, no doubt. Unafraid of the storm and blissfully unaware of the strange woman sleeping in his sons' bedroom closet.

He might as well have been on the moon.

She stretched restlessly, almost wishing she was as happily unconscious of him as he was of her. But she needed him because he made her feel safe.

Why did her demons always come alive when she closed her eyes in the dark?

She hated feeling shut in and alone, and she felt she was—even though the closet door was louvered and her darling boys were just outside, snugly tucked beneath quilts in their bunk beds, oblivious to the storm and her fears. She lay stiffly on her hidden pallet in their huge closet and stared at the ceiling, watching the lightning that flashed through the louvers and caused irregular patterns of blue light to dance across the walls and hanging clothes.

Her strength had returned rapidly, but, so far, not her memory. Vague illusive images from her past seemed to flicker at the edges of her mind like the lightning, their brief flares so brilliant they blinded her before they vanished into pitch blackness.

Her entire world had become Lucas Broderick's coldly modern mansion perched on its bluff above Corpus Christi Bay. But more than the mansion's high white walls and polished marble floors; more than its winding corridors and spiral staircases intrigued her. With every day that passed, she had become more fascinated by Lucas Broderick himself.

From almost that first moment when she had awakened in his sons' closet to their rush of adolescent chatter, they had made her aware of *him*.

"What if Dad finds her?"

An audible gasp and then terrified silence as if that prospect was too awful to contemplate.

"You'd better not let him—stupid."

She had opened her eyes and found their fearful, curious faces peering eagerly at her. She'd had no memory of who they were or how she'd gotten here.

But she'd quickly learned that they were Lucas's adorable sons, and that they looked endearingly like him.

"She's awake."

"Told you she'd live."

"We've got to feed her something or she'll starve like your gerbil."

"What's your name?"

Her name? Blue lights flickered, and she shook her head and made a low moan.

"Pete said she had amnesia, dummy."

Pete? Who was Pete?

"You hungry?"

"Maybe...some broth," she whispered.

Their heads swiveled and they stared at each other in round-eyed consternation as if they'd never heard the word. "Broth?"

"Then water," she managed weakly.

That started a quarrel over who got to fetch it, each of them wanting to.

For ten long days and longer nights those two wonderful boys had fought many battles over the privilege of nursing her. They had checked medical books out of the library. They had cleaned her wounds and doctored them with medicine from Lucas's huge marble bathroom. They had painstakingly picked the slivers of glass from the soles of her feet with tweezers, plunking the jagged bits into a metal bowl. They had soaked her feet in pails of hot water, and she could almost walk without limping.

They took turns pretending to be sick themselves so that one of them could stay home from school with her. They had given her the antibiotics they tricked their uncle into prescribing for them. For the first few nights they'd coaxed their father into buying and cooking the few foods she could keep down—chicken broth, Jell-O and boiled vegetables, which they'd smuggled up to her.

At first she'd been too weak and ill to worry about the way her presence in their home had forced them to deceive their father. But as she'd grown stronger and more attached to her lively, affectionate nurses, she blamed herself for their burgeoning talent at duplicity. Nursing her wasn't the worst of it. They were hard at work on a covert project they called Operation Nanny.

The boys didn't want Lucas to hire a new nanny. "Because," as Peppin explained, "we couldn't fool one of those nosy old bags so easy as Dad. A nanny'd be up here all the time—she'd probably find you the first day."

Thus, every time Lucas informed the boys of a home interview for a prospective nanny, Peppin, who could mimic Lucas's voice to a T, phoned the woman and told her the job had been filled.

At first the girl had been too ill and too grateful and too terrified of being thrown out of the house to care, but now she felt stricken that she had become a corrupting influence on their characters.

Although Peppin and Montague bickered incessantly, they could be an incredible team. During the day, when Lucas was at work, the boys gave her the run of his huge house, with its soaring ceilings and skylights and views of Corpus Christi Bay. One wall of his bedroom was made entirely of glass. Sometimes she would step out onto his balcony and let the tangy sea air ruffle her hair.

Sometimes she showered in his pink marble bathroom that had both an immense enclosed shower and a bathtub as big as a small swimming pool. Sometimes she spent a languid hour buried beneath mountains of foamy bubbles in his tub. Sometimes she would pick out old clothes from his abundant closets to wear. Always she would linger in his room, studying his things, running his slim black comb through her hair and brushing her teeth with his yellow toothbrush. She would open his drawers and run her fingertips over his undershirts and cuff links, marveling that one man could have so much of everything. But what she loved best was lying in his bed and hugging his pillow to her stomach and imagining him there beside her, holding her. She gathered flowers from his gardens and arranged them in crystal vases everywhere, taking special pains with those that she left on the white table beside his bed. It pleased her when he picked a pale yellow rose from that vase and pinned it to the black lapel of his three-piece suit one morning before he rushed to his office.

She tried to think of ways to repay him for all that his boys had done for her. The endless stark hallways of his beautiful house had been strewn with everything from rumpled clothes, baseball bats, soccer gear and Rollerblades to newspapers when she'd arrived. Dirty dishes had overflowed from the white-tiled kitchen counters onto the ebony dining room table.

When she'd gotten better, she'd convinced the boys that maybe their father wouldn't be so anxious to hire a nanny or a housekeeper if he didn't feel the need for one so strongly. She had made a game of cleaning the house.

While they picked up, she would lie on a couch or a chair, perusing the tattered album that contained black-and-white pictures of Lucas's childhood in India, wondering why he'd looked so unhappy as a boy. Wondering why the pictures of India especially fascinated her even as she prodded the boys to pick up.

Every time Peppin or Monty touched something, the rule was that they had to put it where it belonged. She began talking them through the preparation of simple meals, using the cans in the pantry and the frozen dinners in the refrigerator, so that Lucas always came home to a hot meal. At first they complained bitterly, but she just laughed and tried to motivate them by telling them they were learning basic survival skills.

Mostly they went along with her projects because she lavished attention on them. She walked with them on the beach, threw horseshoes with them and played games. The only thing she refused to do was to let them lead her into the tunnel that wound from the garage under the house down to the beach. When they had unlocked the doors to that weird, underground passage, and she had smelled the mustiness of the place, she had felt as if the black gloom was pressing in on her and she was being suffocated.

Ghastly minutes had crawled by before the feeling of claustrophobia subsided.

"I can't go in," she had whispered, clutching her throat, not understanding her terror as she wrenched her hand free of theirs.

"Why?" they asked excitedly, the beams of their flashlights dancing along the wall.

Suddenly she had some memory of being trapped in a box and knowing she was being buried alive. She remembered coughing as dirt sifted through the cracks of her coffin. She remembered kicking and clawing and screaming when the narrow box was black and silent.

"What's wrong?" the boys demanded.

Blue lights flickered, and the memory was gone.

"I—I don't know." She edged away from them toward the open garage doors and brilliant sunlight. "Let's go inside the house . . . and watch a video or something."

How she ached for them when once more they were safely inside and they showed her their home videos and photograph albums with photos that had been taken of their family before the divorce. There were very few pictures of them. The boys told her that their parents had never had time for them, even when they'd been married. It was worse now, though, since their mother had run off and their father kept threatening to send them to military school.

She began to understand that maybe the reason they doted on her was that she was the first adult who ever enjoyed them and made them feel needed.

She encouraged them to go to their father and talk to him. Foolishly she had caused one quarrel between the father and sons by giving some of Lucas's and the boys' clothes to their yardman and his family. After Lucas had caught the poor man in a pair of slacks from one of his custom-made suits from London, he had yelled at the boys for an hour. She had wept for causing all three of them so much pain. But the incident had blown over, and Lucas had bought the slacks back from the man.

She had taken two pictures of Lucas from his albums to keep when she was in the boys' room alone. One was a photograph of him as a man, the other of him as a boy unhappily perched on top of a huge elephant in India.

Lucas kept a box full of articles about himself in the den. She read them all. Apparently Lucas had a professional reputation for toughness and greed. She read that he never made a move unless it was to his financial advantage, that even the women he dated were always rich—as Joan, his first wife, had been. One reporter had likened his predatory nature to that of a barracuda.

The nights when Lucas was at home were difficult because she felt lonely and isolated in the boys' closet, clutching the photographs of Lucas. But the worst hours were those when all the lights in the house were off and she fell asleep, only to have nightmares.

Most nights she would slip into an old chambray shirt of Lucas's. After Peppin shut the louvered closet door for her, she would lie there while either Peppin or Montague read aloud. This week they had been reading a book called *Psychic Voyages* because she had found *Psychic Vampires,* their favorite, too terrifying. She would lie half-listening to the weird and yet compelling stories of people who believed they had lived other lives.

Eventually she would fall asleep, and it was never long before the dreams came—vivid, full-color visions that seemed so real and loomed larger than life.

Tonight was worse, maybe because it had stormed.

She was a little girl again, playing in a sun-splashed rose garden beside a vast white mansion with a dark-haired girl. At first they carefully gathered the roses, filling huge baskets with them. Then her dream changed. The sky filled with dark clouds, and the house was a blackened ruin. There was nothing in the baskets but stems and thorns. She was older, and her companion was gone. Suddenly a fanged monster with olive-black eyes sprang into the ruined rose garden and began chasing her. She knew if he caught her, he would lock her in a box and bury her alive. But as she ran, her speed slowed, and his accelerated, until she felt his hot breath on her neck and his hands clawing into her waist and dragging her into a dark cave. At first she was afraid she'd been buried alive. Then suddenly fire was all around her and she was struggling through the thick suffocating smoke, trying to find her way out. The last thing she saw was a dead man's gray face.

She screamed, a piercing, ear-shattering cry that dragged her back to the lumpy pallet. The louvered door was thrown open instantly, and Peppin's small compact body crouched over hers. His fingers, which smelled of peanut butter and grape jelly and of other flavors best not identified, pressed her lips.

His eyes were big and bright. His thin whisper was colored with excitement. "It's okay. Go back to sleep."

A door down the hall banged open.

Montague whistled from his bed. "Psst! Dad's coming!"

The louvered doors that were yanked together didn't quite close. Peppin scampered to his bed, diving under his covers a second before their door opened.

"Another nightmare, Peppin?"

She lay huddled beneath her blanket, her trembling easing ever so slightly when she heard *his* beautiful voice.

Every night for ten nights her screams had brought him to this room.

The storm had abated, and the night, though still, was held in a humid pall. The worst of the rain had moved out to the gulf, but she could hear the occasional drip of moisture from the eaves.

Even as part of her mind was stampeding in panic, she lifted her head and put her eye to the thread of light that sifted through the slats. The screen saver of the kids' computer gave off a flickering bluish glow. In the charcoal gray shadows of the moonlit room, she could just make out Lucas's tall, broad form silhouetted in the open doorway.

Tonight he was shirtless, and she found herself staring at his bare chest and corded muscles, and at the long white scars that crisscrossed his torso.

Already accustomed to the lack of light, she could see the drowsiness in his silver eyes and the rumpled waves of his inky dark hair that he wore too long for a lawyer. His face was leather-dark and starkly arrogant, yet she sensed he had known pain. He seemed huge and dangerous, uncompromisingly tough and masculine. And yet she felt astonishingly safe with him in the bedroom.

"Yes, Daddy, a really bad nightmare," Peppin said in a breathless, thready voice.

Lucas padded silently across the room, and the mattress groaned as he sat on the edge of his younger son's bed.

"What was the monster like tonight?"

Lucas's drawl had the power to hold her spellbound.

"Oh—he was just awful. He had huge purple eyes just popping out of their sockets. And a tail with green spikes."

"Green spikes?"

She watched Lucas's large pale hand stroke Peppin's hair, and it was almost as if he soothed her with those long, callused fingers.

"You know, Peppin, I've had a few weird dreams lately, too."

"About monsters?"

"No." Lucas's voice softened. "About a girl."

The girl in the closet lay very still. But her breathing accelerated, as did her heartbeats. His words seemed to linger inside her, registering almost hypnotically in that sweet, secret place in her soul.

"The first dream was a nightmare. It was about this girl who was terrified. I wanted to save her but I couldn't. She kept screaming, but when I reached her, it was too late." His voice broke. "She died in my arms. I woke up in a cold sweat. The dream was so vivid. She was so real. I still can't seem to get her out of my mind."

"I'd rather dream about a pretty girl than about a monster with big teeth any night, Dad."

"Big teeth, huh?" Lucas murmured.

Lucas's voice resonated pleasantly along the girl's nerve endings.

"Pointy teeth with silver tips. I was afraid he was going to eat me alive. Or... or maybe suck my blood like a giant vampire." Peppin punctuated this last with a hideous slurping sound.

Lucas's hand continued its gentle strokes. "I'm here, and I'm not going to let anything or anyone into this room."

She closed her eyes, feeling as though Lucas was caressing her and speaking to her, feeling some undeniable powerful attraction to him.

She sighed, wishing she could remember her own nightmare, yet thankful she couldn't.

She ran her fingertips over *his* chambray shirt, hugging the cotton fabric to her skin, liking the way his masculine scent clung to his shirt, and therefore to her.

Lucas.

He didn't even know she existed.

Her chest swelled with some unnamed emotion for him that was more potent than any she'd ever known.

The idea of him obsessed her, consumed her.

The boys thought that if they kept him from hiring a nanny they could keep her existence a secret. But she knew differently. Time was their enemy. Lucas was too smart not to discover her, and when he did, he would probably despise her. Still, she thrilled to the fantasy of their first encounter with every fiber of her being. Even as she dreaded it.

A long time later, Lucas's melodious voice trailed into silence. When he was sure his sons were both asleep, he got up and left.

And later, when she dreamed of the monsters again and of the face with the olive-bright eyes, Lucas was there. Moving with the speed of lightning and scooping her up against his muscled chest, he carried her to safety. And there, far away from danger, he kissed her, his mouth fastening upon hers with greedy, all-consuming passion.

This time when she awoke, she was hot and breathless and so filled with longing for him that she could not suppress the urge to get up and tiptoe quietly down the hall to his room.

His bedroom door was ajar, and his large bed where she had lain and daydreamed about him was awash in moonlight.

Silently she made her way to him.

She gasped when she saw how beautiful he was, sleep having washed the worry from his harsh face. His bronze skin appeared amazingly smooth, unmarred except for the long white scars that ran across his chest. Where had he gotten scars like that?

She had come to ease her longing, but one glance at the sheets molding the tanned sprawl of his huge body only increased her longing for him a hundredfold.

She had been alone so long. *Without him for so long.*

Without him? What made her think she had been with him before? But strangely, she did.

Would he recognize her? Would he be able to tell her who she was?

All she knew was that he did not seem like a barracuda to her. No. To her he was very, very dear.

Her mouth went dry. Her heart ached. Her knees trembled.

Hugging her waist, she sank to the floor beside him, swallowing against the tight constriction in her throat.

She clenched her hands. Never had she wanted anything so much as she wanted to run her fingertips through the thick tumble of black hair on that snowy pillow or let them glide over his wide shoulders.

A great tenderness welled inside her as she studied his bluntly carved features and hard mouth. She remembered her dream and his kiss, and fresh desire raced through her veins. She wanted to taste him, to know him. To belong to him.

And suddenly her loneliness made her hunger for him too much to resist.

Even though she knew it was crazy and an invasion of his privacy, she crawled closer to his bed. There she swept the masses of her yellow hair back with one hand and leaning toward him, carefully brushed her lips against his hair that fell across his brow, next to the dark skin at his temple.

He was as hot as if he had a fever.

And suddenly so was she.

Two kisses. Only two. He was so warm. Instantly her breathing was shallower, raspier. So was his. Instantly she was driven by a nearly overpowering need to trace the shape of his lips with her mouth, to deepen her kisses until he awakened and knew she was there.

He stirred suddenly and groaned. His mouth curved in a sensual white smile, as if he was having a wanton, lascivious dream.

She felt a blinding current of emotion, unlike anything she had ever known, leap from him to her as she jerked away from him.

She had to leave.

But the tantalizing taste of him remained on her lips.

For one long second she closed her eyes and imagined him waking up and finding her. Would he know
her? Would he accept her or reject her? She imagined
him reaching for her, accepting her into his bed, into
his life, telling her that he had always loved her.

Dear God. What was she doing to herself?

Then, terrified he would sense her presence, she sti-
fled a low moan and ran down the hall to the boys'
closet, where she lay sleepless on her pallet, feeling
dissatisfied, aching with new needs and desires.

She couldn't bear to stay in his house another day.

She couldn't bear the thought of ever leaving him.

Three

When his Lincoln slewed overfast onto Ocean Drive, radials whining, Lucas jammed the accelerator down hard. His X-rated dream last night was living proof he'd gone too damn long without a woman. He'd awakened in a sweat again, only this time the gorgeous blonde who'd decided to haunt his dreams of late had climbed into his bed and run her mouth and tongue all over him.

He'd awakened so steamed up he'd driven to his gym to work out before going into his office.

Now he felt hot and sticky and irritable. He'd forgotten the notice in the locker room yesterday about the water being turned off today for plumbing tests.

"What? My fault? How the hell do you mean?" Lucas growled into his cellular phone as he jerked the steering wheel to the right. Palm trees, hot-pink oleander and sparkling views of the bay spurted past in a blur.

Lucas was quickly coming to dislike this Mrs. Peters, the nanny who'd been a no-show yesterday.

His fault? Until she'd said that, he'd been only half listening. He was late, and his mind had been vacillating between the girl who'd tormented his dreams and his nine o'clock appointment with the ever-uptight Stinky Brown.

Stinky was proving to be an impossible client. He had been happy enough when Gertrude's doctor had agreed to testify that the old lady was senile. But Stinky had been going crazy ever since he'd found out about the blackened body in Bethany Ann's burned van. Apparently the girl had told her friends in Mexico that her grandmother had written her about changing the will. She'd also informed them of her grandmother's sudden death and her plan to return to the ranch for her grandmother's memorial service.

Lucas had sent an investigator to Mexico. Ugly gossip was rife about the heiress. Wanted for questioning by the police, Bethany had vanished. Which meant she was probably guilty as sin.

Stinky should have been thrilled. Instead he seemed terrified that the media would get wind of the scandal and blow it all out of proportion. Stinky wanted the girl found and the rumors silenced—fast.

"But Mr. Broderick," came Mrs. Peters's penetrating, dry voice over his phone, "while I am sorry that you came home early expecting to meet me there, you yourself called me yesterday afternoon and told me you'd already hired someone. That is the only reason I didn't show up."

Lucas forced his mind from the missing heiress. An image of a pale Peppin peering at him in the foyer flashed in Lucas's mind. Peppin's voice had been grave. "Mrs. Peters? Why, er, no, Dad. We waited by the phone just like you said. She didn't even call."

"What time did I call you, Mrs. Peters?" Lucas demanded, his stern tone almost convulsing with anger.

"Really, Mr. Broderick, you should know that better—"

Lucas exploded. "What time?"

Stubborn silence from the woman.

Then she said in an exasperated tone, "A little after two. I remember because—"

Lucas didn't give a damn why the blasted woman remembered.

"I didn't call you, Mrs. Peters. I know that because I was in a conference all afternoon."

"Oh. Then who—"

"Never mind."

"Do you want to reschedule the interview?"

When hell freezes over, lady. Lucas said a clipped goodbye and hung up.

"Damn!" Lucas was coldly furious with himself for not figuring out before now that Peppin and Montague had had something to do with the six nannies who'd stood him up.

For eleven miraculous days the boys had been so good he'd been tempted to check their shoulder blades to see if they'd sprouted wings.

Why hadn't he been more suspicious of that eerie feeling that some unseen angel had moved into his home and was making his life with his sons magically better?

His mind flashed back, struggling to interpret the bizarre events of late. First, he remembered that odd experience in the Moran foyer when he'd felt—there was no other word—haunted.

No, he had told himself to forget that. With great effort he forced the intriguing episode from his mind and thought instead about the changes in the household since he'd returned to Corpus Christi.

The boys had been pleasant, companionable, thoughtful and neat. They'd fixed several meals for him. In fact, ever since San Antonio, Lucas's home life had been downright idyllic. Aside from his concern over his sons' fevers, queasy stomachs, nightmares and absences from school, aside from that act of bizarre generosity when they'd given the yardman two of his best suits, this was the one week since Peppin's birth that being with his sons had been almost a joy.

Lucas grew increasingly puzzled as he remembered them asking him to show them how to boil broth and vegetables—even broccoli. Other than French fries and onion rings, they'd never eaten a damned vegetable in their lives. Why, they'd never touched broccoli with so much as the tip of a fork.

And all those medical questions. All those calls to Pete. Damn it. Why?

Lucas wasn't the only person they'd duped. Pete had prescribed a light diet, antibiotics and bed rest.

What had the brats really done with those pills and vegetables and bowls of soup they'd pretended to gobble down? Lucas frowned as he remembered how they'd tracked back and forth to their room with those endless bowls of broth and vegetables.

And then it hit him.

They were feeding something up there. Something large and ravenous that was either badly injured or diseased.

Vegetables ruled out anything as remotely attractive as a large dog.

It had to be something so repulsive they were sure he would never let them keep it. And why had Peppin awakened him every night screaming? Had the creature gotten loose in the house? Were they scared of it?

Damn it! *What were they hiding up there?*

Lucas switched on the radio, only to turn it off instantly when the newscaster began an update on the serial murders of several Texas lawyers. Some maniac was shooting lawyers in their homes in an execution-style manner. The story was making headlines all over the state, and his partners and staff attorneys hadn't been able to talk of anything else since a Houston associate had been found shot in the head in his backyard.

Hot-pink oleander blossoms waved airily above the high white wall that hid all but the top story of Lucas's mansion from the boulevard. Lucas swerved through the gigantic gates past the Realtor's For Sale sign, which had been erected shortly after the divorce.

Lucas had little liking for his three-story, ultra-modern, glass-tiled monstrosity with its elaborate security system, tennis courts, pool, Jacuzzi, boathouse, docks, fishing pier and servants' quarters, all of which were Joan's exorbitantly priced creations.

Lucas had grown up in small houses and felt lost in the large, overdecorated rooms. The place had become an albatross around his neck. The Realtor kept giving him lists of necessary repairs, and the first item on every list was to seal the ancient tunnel beneath his house that led to the bay. The tunnel was a curious relic from the turn-of-the-century mansion Joan had bought at great expense and torn down to build their home.

The Lincoln jerked to a stop at the massive house, and Lucas jumped out. Even before he opened the front doors, he could hear rap music pouring from his boys' room in a tidal wave of jivy drumbeats.

Good. The little savages were home. For once their music served some purpose other than to drive him crazy. He could use the pounding beat as a cover to sneak up on them.

He raced up the winding staircase and down the hall, past his bedroom, noting that his shower was on. How many times had he told them to use their own?

When he reached their closed door, he listened outside for a moment. Then, without knocking, he flung it open and charged inside.

Rap music pulsed from two immense speakers.

"We're all going to be stone deaf," he yelled as he rushed toward the amplifier and jerked three plugs from the wall.

The sound of the running tap from his bathroom could be heard in the deafening silence that followed, which was odd, because both boys were already dressed for school. Peppin, who was patting pale powder all over his face and smudging eyeshadow under his eyes with a Kleenex, jumped guiltily.

"D-Dad? How come you're— You're home!" he squeaked, his eyes darting to Montague.

Lucas picked up the boxes of powder and eye shadow and pitched them in the trash in disgust. "So—you're not really sick!" He paused. "I talked to Mrs. Peters."

Montague, who was sprawled on the floor reading a booklet entitled *Step by Step: How To Make Awesome IDs* while he laced up his combat boots, wisely kept his eyes glued to a page that dealt with the many uses of laser copiers.

"I want to know what the hell you two have been up to!"

"N-nothing, Dad."

Lucas's hard gaze flicked away from Peppin's chalk-white face. Today, as of late, their room was abnormally tidy, and there was no sign of their large, repulsive pet. No stale scent of droppings, urine or old food. Not so much as a paper or a book on the floor. Only one stray horseshoe.

A bouquet of plump pink roses adorned Montague's desk. Now that was odd, because Lucas couldn't remember either of his sons ever so much as looking at flowers, let alone picking them and arranging them in a vase. Suddenly Lucas was remembering that roses were all over the house. In fact, there was a vase of white roses beside his bed.

Did the pet give off some peculiar odor the flowers masked?

Lucas stalked to the closet and threw open the doors, but he saw nothing other than a rumpled sheet, two photographs of himself, a blanket and the favorite old chambray shirt he'd been looking for.

The animal's bedding? He snatched up his shirt.

Furious, Lucas turned to them. "Where is it?"

"What, Dad?" Montague's voice was calm, but his hands had frozen on the tangled laces of his second boot.

"Damn it. Your new pet."

Peppin made a low choking sound. "P-pet?"

"Where is whatever you've been feeding all that chicken soup to? *What is going on?* You've played sick, behaved yourselves, cleaned house, cooked supper—all to put me off my guard."

In the silence, he heard his shower, really heard it.

"Dad, we're going to be late for school. Could you give us a ride—"

Late was a buzz word. Lucas glanced at his watch and remembered Stinky Brown.

Through gritted teeth, he said, "I'm going to shower. We'll talk on the way to school."

The boys stared at him white-faced. "D-Dad. No. We can explain—everything. Right now."

"I've run out of time—now. It'll have to wait."

He was vaguely pleased that the boys looked so cowed. If he couldn't resolve the issue in the car, with any luck at all, they would talk to their friends and find a new home for whatever it was, and the problem would have solved itself by the time he got home tonight.

"You two had better be ready when I am." Lucas began stripping as he stalked away from them toward his bedroom.

Peppin raced after him. "But, Dad—"

Lucas whirled. "Yeah? What's with this sudden willingness to confess?"

"Dad, I—I was going to take a shower—"

"Use your own bathroom."

For once Montague, whose black-booted feet looked amazingly large, had come after him, too. "Hey, Dad, maybe you could use our shower—"

"Suddenly everybody wants to talk and keep me out of my shower." Lucas yanked his running shorts off. "Well, too bad. I'm stark naked and I've run out of time and patience with your games."

As he strode through his bedroom into his steamy bathroom, he thought he heard Peppin say rather uneasily, "Cool it, Monty. Didn't he say he wanted to meet our new pet?"

"So?"

"Chill out. This could work."

What could work?

"Maybe they'll dig each other."

"You're stupid."

"It *could* happen."

Clouds of steam were pouring out of his overlarge shower as Lucas yanked the door open and stepped onto the pink marble that was slippery with soap.

Lucas shut his eyes as the warm water hit his face full force. Automatically he grabbed for the bar of soap in his soap dish, but it wasn't there.

Then soft warm fingers placed a bar that smelled of roses in his right hand.

"Thanks," he said as he began to soap the nape of his neck.

It took him a second to get it.

He wasn't alone.

His hand stopped scrubbing.

His eyes snapped open, and she was there—stepping out of the pink mists behind him like a naked goddess from the wildest adolescent fantasy he'd ever had, like Venus rising from that shell in the sea in that painting he'd seen in Florence.

He knew her.

Her blue eyes flashed with recognition, too.

High cheekbones. Yellow hair. Model-slim. Gorgeous. Skin as creamy as alabaster.

She was an exact replica of the girl who had come to him in his dreams. She was the girl of his nightmare, as well as the girl who'd gotten friendlier and friendlier in every dream since until the one last night when she'd crawled on top of him and teased him until he was insane with desire.

Was he dreaming now? Or was she for real?

For no particular reason he allowed himself to remember the spooky feeling he'd gotten when he'd walked out of the Moran library and he'd felt so positive that someone was watching him. Only there hadn't been anybody there. And yet he had felt as if some alien spirit who was very powerful and very sweet had connected to his soul. For a few blissful seconds he'd felt unleashed, set free from all his cynicism and bitterness. Torrents of blocked and longed-for feelings had flowed out of him. He still was at a loss to explain it.

Then there were the dreams about the blonde. And suddenly here she was. In the flesh.

This was crazy. Too crazy to believe.

"Hello?" came her velvet voice beneath his ear.

She was real.

He blinked once, twice, and she was still there. Her eyes sparkled. She was lovelier than ever—and as naked as the day she was born. He inhaled the scent of roses.

For a week he had been haunted by that scent. And now he knew why. It was her scent.

He felt like Adam finding his Eve.

He felt that every moment in his life had been leading to this one.

Funny—even as his eyes locked with hers, even as he carefully forced himself not to lower them, even as he forced himself to concentrate on the way her black lashes were clumped together with dewdrops of moisture around her incredibly blue eyes, he still saw everything.

Shampoo suds spilled from her throat and clung in foamy white mounds to her nipples.

She was built, really built, with high, shapely breasts, a gently rounded belly, a narrow waist and smooth legs that went on forever. Her lips parted in a tender half smile, and he saw that she had a slight gap between her two front teeth. And Lucas, who had been an English major in college, remembered Chaucer saying that was an indication of a sensual nature.

Did she give off a glow? Was that why he felt so dazzled?

As if in a daze, he remembered Peppin's cryptic remark. *Didn't he say he wanted to meet our new pet?*

Maybe they'll dig each other.

Thus far, she hadn't cried out or made any sound at all—maybe she was as stunned as he.

Or maybe—how did he know this?—she'd been expecting this moment, too.

Slowly Lucas raised his hands above his head, as if in mock surrender—to show her he wouldn't touch her or hurt her or molest her in any way.

But it wasn't necessary—because, amazingly, she really wasn't afraid of him. She was the first to let her eyes travel boldly from his face down his bronze flexing chest muscles, which were matted with dark, crinkly hair, down the length of his flat, tapering stomach and the rest of his lean body. Then she looked at him where his tan line stopped with the same intense curiosity and lack of modesty. It was as if they were already lovers and she had a right to do so. Her eyes continued to touch him intimately. Pulsations of liquid heat raged through him.

He flushed at her saucy impudence and then hastily pushed the shower door open, cursing as he stumbled backward so fast he stubbed his big toe on the shower door. In between grunts of pain, he hopped toward the rack and grabbed a towel.

Where the hell had Peppin and Montague found her?

"Boys!" he shouted as he bunched the thick white terry cloth around his waist. Then, louder, "Boys!"

They were far too clever to answer.

She turned off the faucets and said quietly, "I'm sorry if you hurt your toe." And then, "It's not their fault, you know."

"Don't defend them." A pause. "Who the hell are you?" Lucas whispered, hotly aware of her lithe golden body. "How long have you been living—"

But he already knew. "Eleven days?" he croaked, his answer sounding choppy and thick-tongued.

Her face turned crimson. She nodded. "I wanted to meet you, but I was afraid—"

She was the pet. She was the mysterious angelic presence he'd sensed in the house who'd magically improved his life with his sons. Her spell was so powerful she'd even managed to insert herself into his dreams.

No wonder the boys had been determined to fire all those nannies and stay home and tend her.

The girl stepped out of the stall, her blue eyes shining through the mists, her wet hair glued in tangles to her shoulders.

Lucas observed a neatly stitched pink line along her hairline as he roughly pitched her a towel. For no reason at all he remembered Peppin bombarding Pete with all those medical questions. He had felt such fatherly pride at the seductive dream that maybe, after all, Peppin might really amount to something and become a doctor.

His aim was off, and the towel fell to the floor. He leaned down and picked it up, and as he held it out to her, his hands accidentally touched hers. He felt the silken heat of her soft skin, and his heart beat faster.

Her reaction to him was equally intense, although she, too, attempted to hide it, not that she was any better at it than he. For he saw that her hands trembled as she wrapped the towel around herself, and that once it was snugly secured above her breasts, he saw that they trembled, too, as if she was breathing irregularly.

What the hell was going on here?

Never in his entire life had he felt so powerfully drawn to another human being.

Never before had he met a stranger and felt he already knew her.

She hadn't bothered to dry herself properly, and heated rivulets of water and soap oozed down her skin and pooled beside her bare feet.

She kept staring at him, the pupils of her eyes so drastically dilated that only a ring of blue fire seemed to encircle them. "I wish I knew who I was," she replied honestly in a small, frightened voice that undid him. "If I knew, maybe I'd know where I belonged and I'd have already gone. I—I thought maybe you could tell me."

"Me? How the hell would I know?"

"But you looked at me as if you know me."

He stared at her feet because it seemed the safest thing about her to look at. There were ugly scratches on her slim ankles.

She had tiny feet.

He lifted his gaze and studied that fresh pink scar at her hairline. There were tiny scratches on her cheek. For no reason at all he remembered tiny bloody footprints across a white tile floor. Next he remembered Peppin's first medical question had been in that hospital parking lot.

And then Lucas knew.

Again he saw the dangling IV above those blood-spattered sheets in the examining room.

This girl was Pete's patient.

This glorious angel with the soapsuds in her hair who had invaded his house and made him a happy man was the escaped dope addict. She could be anybody.

There was only one thing to do.

He had to call Pete.

"Get dressed," he said curtly. "Then we'll talk."

"Yes, Lucas."

Lucas.

His name. Just his name. So familiar and yet so...erotically alien. Her husky velvet voice had made it into something indescribably precious.

The adoring quality in her voice did strange things to him. He felt ten years younger and all the logical, self-serving rules he had lived by were shattered.

He felt her silent plea. *Tell me who I am.*

Damn, people couldn't talk to each other without words.

He felt turned on by her. And ridiculously safe. As if he'd come home from a long journey to the one person in the entire universe he wanted to spend all eternity with.

Which was absolutely absurd.

He had no bond with her. She didn't give a damn about anything except using him. She was just some troublesome stranger, a runaway, a doper, maybe. She had invaded his house, tricked his sons into betraying him—

The house sparkled. She had cooked meals for him. Brought roses to him. Roses that he had worn all day, the scent of which had haunted him.

He remembered how badly the boys had taken his finding a new home for their pet Doberman pinscher who'd bitten the postman and chased all the neighbor kids. They liked this girl a whole lot more than they'd liked Kaiser.

So did he.

Lucas reminded himself that she was a worse liability than Kaiser could have been, that he had to get rid of her as soon as possible.

"Get dressed," he repeated, but in a gentler tone to put her off guard.

Her smile died.

As she stared into his eyes, he had the unsettling sensation that she had zapped into his brain and read every single dark intention and suspicion he had concerning her.

"Please don't send me away," she said.

"You can't stay here."

Her warm, frightened eyes met his again. "If you throw me out, they'll find me and kill me."

Two heartbeats. His and hers. As a grander emotion flared into being.

"Who will kill you?"

"I—I don't know."

No way could he let anything happen to her.

"I want to stay here with you," she said, her gaze and voice warm.

This time it was he who read her mind.

She wanted him to seize her, to wrap her in his arms and pull her down to the marble floor, to make swift violent love to her, while they were still flushed and steaming from the shower.

She wanted him to love her. Forever.

This whole damn thing was too much. Way too much. Crazy, in fact.

"Hold me," she whispered in a barely audible voice. "Just hold me."

"Later."

"No."

Maybe he could have walked away from her if she hadn't smiled so sheepishly and charmingly. If the towel above her breasts hadn't shifted that fraction of an inch lower.

If they hadn't both reached to keep it from falling.

If their fingertips hadn't touched.

If they both hadn't laughed nervously.

If her laughter hadn't died in that breathless hush. "You want this as much as I do."

"What?"

She smiled sexily and reached up and stroked his wet hair.

"This," she said huskily, winding a black strand around a fingertip. "And... And everything."

If her innocent glances and caresses stung him like flame, what would the full tide be?

Strange, how he felt he already knew.

Her warm knowing gaze locked with his and drew him inside her, fusing all that was holy and all that was not to her shining spirit.

He was a hardened man who had had many women.

He had been badly burned by the one woman he had loved and married.

But this was different.

Utterly and completely different.

And ten thousand times more dangerous.

He could no more resist her than a swimmer could resist the force of a dangerous tidal current.

As he drew her into his arms, wanting her soul as well as her body, he felt a thunderstorm of unreasoning, inexplicable emotions.

For a long moment he savored the sweetness of pressing her resplendent soft damp flesh against himself.

Very slowly, very gently he lowered his mouth to hers.

His kiss was neither hard nor long, but it vibrated inside them both with deep, underlying tenderness and awakened them to shattering, never-felt-before needs.

He would never have believed that a single kiss could hold the power to change him—forever.

"Who are you?" he whispered again, frantic at the speed of this thing, even as he gave her the gentlest smile he had ever given any woman. "Where did you come from? Why?"

"I—I don't know. I just know that I feel I've known you before."

"I've never set eyes on you till today. Believe me. You're not somebody I could forget." He wasn't ready to admit to her that he had dreamed about her.

She gave him an uncertain look that said she didn't quite believe him.

Amnesia, he reminded himself. She had amnesia. She could be anybody. She could be married. What if there was—

Suddenly he was terrified of all the horrendous possibilities.

God. No. He couldn't bear the thought of another man possessing her, touching her. Or of her loving someone else.

His grip tightened around her waist.

He would cross those bridges later—if it came to that.

Now she was his. Totally and completely his.

He kissed her again, harder, in a fury to stake his right of possession.

But it wasn't necessary. With every answering kiss, she told him that she was already his and would always be his.

He panicked, afraid of where this was taking him, but he couldn't stop kissing her even when tears spilled from her lashes as she kissed him back just as fearfully.

Four

Lucas's spacious L-shaped office—done in dramatic marble and pale parquet floors and furnished with Oriental rugs and antique porcelains—exuded understated wealth and power.

Stinky stared at Lucas hard. His voice was measured and deliberate. "Frankly, I expected more from someone with your ruthless, hard-boiled reputation. You haven't done a damn thing."

Lucas's jaw tightened at the slur, but his gaze didn't waver. "Because what you want isn't in your best interests. You say the cops have a murder weapon and they've found drugs in the burned van and more drugs in one of her partially built houses in Mexico. An eyewitness says she was at the wheel of the van when it hit that other car and rolled. The police think she was trying to find a place to dump Miguel Santos's body.

He was her driver. You ought to like the way this thing is heating up. The longer Bethany's on the run, the worse it will be for her.''

''Exactly. That's why you have to find her.''

''But—''

''Chandra couldn't be involved in drug-running or murder.''

''I'm not talking about innocence or guilt.''

Stinky's bloodshot black eyes narrowed as he leaned forward. The heavy scent of cologne wafted with him, as did the fainter odor of booze.

It was early yet, but Stinky had already had a drink or two. Maybe more.

Stinky had plenty of surface charm. Most women probably found his rugged body and his classically handsome face perfect. He had reddish-brown hair with a widow's peak and a chin with a deep cleft in it. In his dark, custom-made suit, he had the sleek, pampered look of a movie star playing a rich businessman. But neither acting nor business was his trade. Lucas had researched the man. One way or another, Stinky had always made his living off wealthy women.

''No, counselor. We're talking about life or death—Chandra's.''

''You're trying to tell me your only concern here is for her welfare?''

Lucas's dark brows arched cynically as Stinky sank back into his leather chair and began rummaging in his briefcase. His trembling tanned hand closed around a file folder, pulled it out and thumbed through it. With a tight smile, Stinky tossed it onto Lucas's desk.

"What—" As Lucas opened the folder, three eight-by-ten glossy photographs of a beautiful blonde fell out.

Stinky grabbed them and spread them face up on top of Lucas's papers. "I ask you—is this the face of a killer?"

Lucas was about to argue that that was hardly the point, but as he lifted a photograph, he found himself staring into a pair of vivacious blue eyes that drank too deeply of his soul.

Oh, my God—

His tongue thickened. Had his life depended upon it, he couldn't have uttered a word.

He was stunned that even a mere picture of *her* generated that strange, awesome power over him.

Panic began to rise in Lucas as he studied the scintillatingly luxuriant yellow hair, the inviting lips that were parted in laughter, the flawless, full-bosomed, slender-hipped figure.

Chandra Moran was the girl he'd met naked in his shower less than an hour ago. The girl whose lips he'd kissed. The girl who'd haunted his every waking thought and had even haunted his dreams for days.

So—this was what she looked like in full glory when she was happy and unafraid and completely healthy. When her skin was golden from the sun.

She was really something. Hell, as if he didn't already know that.

In another shot her hands were splayed open on her hips as she stood halfway up the gray steps of a Mayan pyramid. In tight jeans and a halter top, with her golden hair streaming in the wind, laughing at her photographer, she looked younger and more carefree than she had looked in his shower. In another photo she had laid her head on a sacrificial stone chopping block and was sticking out her tongue at the camera as if she was taunting her executioner.

Fully clothed, she was every bit as sexy as she was naked.

Cute butt. Long legs. The three pictures were all it took to make Lucas's desire for her well up. Only now she had a name, a very dangerous name. Now his desire for her was laced with fear and danger because he had a head full of questions that he was suddenly afraid to ask.

His hands clenched, wrinkling the edges of the photos before he dropped them on his desk. He knew he was behaving stupidly, that he had to say something fast. Somehow he managed a hoarse whisper.

"This is . . . Bethany Ann Moran?"

Stinky's hard, bright eyes locked with his. "I'll grant you, she's a looker."

Reluctantly Lucas forced a disinterested nod. "I imagined her differently. More like a straight-laced nun or a schoolteacher type."

"Not our Chandra. She's had dozens of wild boyfriends."

Lucas flushed, angry at the mention of other men.

"I was her first." Stinky reddened, too. "She dumped me."

"Why?"

"None of your damned business. You just find her, counselor, before the wrong guy does."

"You mean—the cops?"

"Not necessarily."

The only ethical response was to admit he already had her. But as he watched Stinky rise from his chair, some raw, gut-level instinct stopped Lucas.

The silence between the two men lengthened and grew strangely uncomfortable, at least for Lucas.

"You okay, counselor? You seem kind of nervous all of a sudden."

Lucas finger-combed his inky hair and tried to act casual. "Worked late. Big new project. Very big."

"Hope it won't distract you from Bethany."

"Oh, er, no chance of that."

"Good."

Stinky's black eyes fastened on Lucas as Lucas hastily jumped up and ushered him to the door.

The minute Stinky was gone, Lucas canceled the rest of his morning's appointments to consider this new information.

Bethany Ann Moran was living in *his* house. She had been in a car wreck. She had been brought to the hospital with head injuries; she'd also been high on drugs. She was wanted by the police. His own kids had played savior and doctor.

The legal ramifications of not giving her up were horrendous. If anything happened to her, her family could sue him for every dime he had. He didn't want to think about the police. Then there were the financial aspects. He would lose his shot at the Moran will.

So be it.

Was she or wasn't she innocent? Was someone trying to kill her? Until he knew more, Lucas had to protect her.

What the hell had really happened in that accident? Lucas couldn't believe Chandra had murdered

Santos, her driver, and had planned to dump his body somewhere.

So, damn it, what had happened?

He got up and went to a window. His office was on the seventeenth floor and commanded a view of the bay. In no way did the brilliant sunshine and clear blue sky reflect the growing darkness of his mood.

He went back to his desk and ran his hands through his hair. Suddenly he remembered something that had seemed insignificant at the time.

There had been a van at the Moran ranch. A blue van with a dark man in a Stetson waiting patiently in it while the sky turned black. The van had still been there when he'd driven away from the mansion.

But not the driver.

Lucas's mind raced.

He remembered that he'd felt a strange empathy for Chandra even when he'd been in the library. Then, when he'd stepped into the foyer, he'd sensed that weird connection to some powerful otherworldly presence.

He had felt Chandra.

Chandra had been there.

He knew it in his bones.

That night in San Antonio he had that nightmare about her that had kept him up till dawn.

God.

Had she been in trouble, crying out for help? Had he somehow sensed it? This whole thing kept getting weirder and weirder.

Lucas phoned his top private investigator, Tom Robard, and told him to come over. When Robard got there, Lucas spit out rapid-fire demands. He wanted to know everything about Chandra Moran. Everything about every other Moran, too. Everything about anyone living on the Moran ranch or on the Moran payroll, as well. Everything about Casas de Cristo and the people who ran it. And the investigation had to be kept hush-hush. Lucas had Robard send two bodyguards out to his own house to make sure nobody could get to Bethany, and to make sure she couldn't wander away, either.

Lucas was about to go home when he remembered he still hadn't called Pete.

The answering service said Pete was tied up in surgery.

Damn.

Later.

As Lucas hung up, a woman with a cap of shiny dark hair, a nervous young staff attorney in a black suit, stopped by his office.

"I was wondering if you'd heard, Mr. Broderick?"

Lucas looked up and saw that she was pale and had a dazed look in her eyes. Which meant trouble.

Wearily he shook his head.

"A guy claiming to be the serial killer phoned our office and said you're next."

"Good God. Just what I need."

Five

Lucas froze as he got out of his car and heard his sons' excited shouts, quickly followed by peals of warm, feminine laughter. He heard the clang of a heavy iron horseshoe against an iron stake. And Peppin's triumphant cry as he pitched another horseshoe.

His sons.

Her laughter.

She even sounded beautiful.

The three of them seemed so happy together as they played behind the house somewhere near the pool.

Lucas caught his breath. Drugs? Murder? Could such a gorgeous, innocent-looking woman be capable of such heinous—

Then he remembered Joan. Joan, who had lied to him with a smile. Joan, who had neglected and aban-

doned her own sons. Joan, who had been so undeni-
ably beautiful and passionate in his bed but in so many
others, as well—even that of his best friend.

Bitterly, Lucas wished he was wrong about Chandra, and if she was truly evil, that he could exorcise her
from his fevered brain and heart before it was too late.

She emitted another silvery peal of laughter that
tugged at his heart.

It was already too late.

He loved her.

And so did his sons.

The foundations of his logical life were crumbling.
He could feel everything he'd worked so long and so
hard for going down the tubes, even his career, and
there wasn't a damn thing he could do about it. If
Joan had gutted him and left him for dead, this girl
might be about to deliver the coup de grace.

Warily he prowled around to the back of his white
mansion where he found Peppin, his outstretched
hand still in the air as he watched the horseshoe he'd
flung arc high against the darkening opalescent sky
before falling, ringing the iron stake with an awesome
clatter. Chandra clapped as the boys ran to gather up
their horseshoes.

"Hello—again." Lucas's deep cynical drawl
sounded lazy, but he felt as tightly strung as piano
wire.

Chandra, who was standing against a mass of
fuchsia-colored bougainvillea, whirled, her face
flushing with delight when she saw him. Tiny blue
flames began to blaze in her eyes as hotly as bonfires.
A similar answering excitement coiled warmly around
his heart.

She was so beautiful. He held his breath, his eyes unable to leave her face. He stood motionless, as one enchanted. She dominated his field of vision with her yellow hair gleaming as brightly as pure gold.

In that sparkling moment all his doubts melted away, and she was everything to him. He had missed her acutely in the brief hours they'd been apart.

He was too cold and too cynical and too smart to feel this way.

He was inflamed by her beauty and caught by the sweetness of her fragile smile and radiant face as she looked at him.

With that bright hair falling softly around her shoulders, she was a vision in his old chambray shirt and Peppin's too-tight jeans. He was heartened that the shadows beneath her eyes were lighter and that her cheeks were rosier. One look was enough to tell him that no matter how he fought it, he would never be released from the hold she had on him.

Still, he raged against it inwardly.

She stiffened and grew shy of him, too, somehow sensing the exact moment he started to recoil from her.

Two sea gulls swooped down, fighting for a tidbit of fish, circling, squawking. Distracted by the birds, she laughed nervously.

Peppin picked up one of four huge, bulging plastic garbage bags. "Hey, Dad, look what we did!" Peppin dropped the bag and pointed toward three other overflowing bags lined neatly in front of the pool house.

"She hid a treasure on the beach under a piece of driftwood. She said we were pirates who couldn't remember where we'd buried our treasure and we had to pick up trash while we looked for it," Montague explained.

The beach was constantly littered with bottles, foam cups, plastic bags, boards with rusty nails, pieces of fishing equipment—every imaginable sort of debris that could be thrown overboard from fishing boats or swept from the city streets via the storm sewers.

"That's great. Just great," Lucas said grumpily. Usually the boys threw tantrums at the prospect of picking up so much as a single bottle cap. Lucas resented having still another fresh reason to admire her.

"I have supper waiting," she said, her slanting eyes having grown warily hurt.

"Let's go inside, then," he said. It was all he could manage.

It was a first—the four of them eating together— and she had worked hard to make it special. Dinner was a warm, golden, candlelit affair in his normally white, sterile dining room. She'd had the boys set the table with a melon-colored cloth and matching napkins. Roses scented the room from a crystal vase. Romantic piano music tinkled faintly—Schubert. She had cooked a roast and mashed potatoes and green beans. She'd even made flan— Peppin's favorite.

His, too.

How had she known?

Why was he even surprised? She seemed to know everything about him.

He watched her avoid the beef and pick at her vegetables, while he ate lustily. The roast, which she had flavored with garlic and delicate spices, seemed to melt in his mouth.

The boys chattered about some redheaded friend named Jeremiah who had been sent to the principal's office three times that day. The adults nodded, speaking only when necessary and only to the boys, although each was acutely conscious of the other.

Lucas's tension grew as he sensed the boys watching the two of them, especially him. Finally Peppin, who could never be quiet for long if he was bothered by something, blurted out the question foremost on everybody's mind. "Are you going to be mean to her like you were to Mom and make her go away?"

Like you were to Mom? Was that how they saw it?

"Or can she stay?"

All three of them peered at him in the flickering candlelight. Even in the golden light Chandra was ashen, her gaze wide and frightened, like a doe at bay, not wanting to pressure him and yet pressuring him more than the boys' dark avid faces.

"I hadn't thought much about it."

Liar.

Lucas cut off a piece of roast, inserted it into his mouth and began to chew methodically.

"We like her, Dad," Montague asserted.

"You don't know one damn thing about her." Lucas kept his gaze on his potatoes, but he felt the betrayal she felt when he uttered that lie.

Damn it. He didn't believe in extrasensory perception or whatever this weird bond was between them.

"We know all we need to know, Dad," Peppin said. "She's pretty and nice...and patient. She fits in. And she says she likes you a lot."

"Thank you, Peppin." She flushed. "But I really don't think—"

"And," Peppin continued, "she listens when we talk. She doesn't raise her voice when she gets mad. She doesn't just shout orders and treat us like children. She makes us mind, too. She senses what we want or need to do even before we do."

Incredibly, it was all too true. She had woven her spell on them all. Lucas speared another piece of roast and jammed it defiantly into his mouth. Again it melted on his tongue.

"So—how long do you expect this cozy arrangement to last?" he asked Peppin between succulent bites.

"She's already done a better job and lasted longer than any of the nannies or housekeepers *you* hired," Montague said.

"That might not be so true if you two hadn't sabotaged—"

"We want to keep her, Dad."

She said nothing, but he felt her soul-to-soul plea even more powerfully than either of his sons'.

Please, Lucas, just for a little while.

Okay. Okay, he shot back at her, using ESP just to see if she was tuned into his frequency, too.

Bingo.

Cheeks glowing, her bright gaze lifted to his, and she smiled in astonishment and pleasure as she read his mind.

Her pleasure filled him, saturated him, thrilled him.

This was weird, he thought vaguely, right before he thundered, "All right! You win! She can stay!" He shoved his chair back, stunned. "But that's only because I can't fight everybody."

He got up, furious at himself, at her, at all of them, and stalked to his liquor cabinet, where he made a martini. He tossed it down and made another. With a grimace he tossed that one down, as well, and poured and stirred still another.

"Lucas—"

He turned, his face harshly intense. "You got what you wanted."

"But did you?" she asked in a concerned voice.

She really did sound as if she cared about his happiness more than her own.

He contemplated her beautiful upturned face, and despised himself for the ridiculous, crazy, youthful elation he felt at the mere sight of her. The bitterness and the anger that were always in his heart had all but vanished.

"Yes and no."

"I want to thank you," she said very softly.

When she reached out and put a hand on his sleeve, he jerked convulsively from even that slight touch, mostly because it pleased him almost beyond bearing.

"Don't," he growled as his hands began to shake.

"Don't what?"

"You can stay, but I want you to leave me alone."

"Why? I—I thought—"

"Because I don't understand this thing between you and me. Because I don't like feeling compelled every time I look at you or hear your voice. Because I don't like feeling like a teenager—driven, not myself. Because . . . just because this whole crazy thing is happening too damn fast. I'm not myself when you're around. Nothing like this has ever happened to me before. I don't trust it. I feel like we're getting in too deep."

"Okay. I guess it isn't fair to expect— I mean, I've had eleven days to get used to you," she said simply, reasonably. "To get used to the idea of loving you."

"Don't even say that stupid word. Love doesn't happen this fast."

"I didn't know there were rules."

"Well, there damn well should be."

"I think I've felt this way forever."

"Do you know how ridiculous you sound?" He whirled on her, hating himself when the color drained from her face. "How do you know what you feel when you don't even know who you are?"

"Because I know what I feel in my heart," she said brokenly.

"Damn it. No—"

"Lucas, I do. I had a dream about us last night. I had to leave you, and you were terrified I was abandoning you. You didn't believe me when I said I'd come back."

Odd, her dreaming that. His big fear about love always had to do with the fear of losing it. He felt that way now about her.

Silently, moodily, he mixed another martini, disbelieving her. Disbelieving this whole damn situation.

"Haven't you had enough to drink for one night?" she asked in a wifely tone, which he didn't like.

"Way too much," he agreed pleasantly as he downed the martini. "And way too much of this impossible conversation."

"I'm sorry—"

"This is a big place. You keep to your part of the house. I'll keep to mine." With that he stormed outside.

After he talked to the bodyguards, he went down the narrow path on the bluff to the beach. He stomped mindlessly across the wet sand, not caring that his good Italian dress shoes sank deeply into the stuff. He hurled a few flat shells, sending them skimming across the dark water before he felt her watching him and glanced at the house.

Every window was ablaze. She was standing in one, staring out at him as he'd known she'd be. Her voluptuous beauty drew him like a beacon. More than anything, he wanted to quit fighting her and go to her.

He began to walk fast, his long strides carrying him away from the tall white house and the woman with the golden hair, but not from the confusion burning in his heart.

Impossible relationships were his special talent. It had been love at first sight with Joan, he remembered bitterly.

But he hadn't ever felt like this, a tiny voice that he didn't care to listen to said. He hadn't even slept with this girl, but she had an intuitive grip on his heart and soul that Joan had never achieved even after years of marriage.

An hour later, when he returned, his dark hair ruffled from the wind, his mood only marginally lighter, Chandra was listening to a musical and singing about raindrops on roses while she washed dishes. Her golden hair was tousled, loose tendrils falling around her rosy, flushed cheeks. The sight of her at his sink and the sound of her happy, lilting voice filled him with more of that strange, intense emotion.

Shakily he forced himself to stay safely on the opposite side of the kitchen from her.

She made easy idle conversation, telling him what was on television that he might like, telling him that his kids were upstairs doing their homework.

"Amazing," he muttered, opening the refrigerator and taking out a cola. "I—I think I'll go check on them."

Anything to avoid her.

"Lucas—" Her husky voice and luminous eyes begged him to stay just a little while longer.

He tore his briefcase from the counter and dashed upstairs.

The kids' computer was off. Monty really was rechecking Peppin's math. They were working together—productively, happily.

Another first.

"She's a good cook, isn't she, Dad?" Peppin asked.

"The best," Monty concurred, glancing up slyly from the math textbook.

Lucas had come upstairs to forget her. In a hard voice, he said, "Guys, you won."

"But you're being mean to her, Dad. She was crying in the kitchen a while ago."

Lucas winced, remembering the haunted vagueness in her eyes when he'd told her he was leaving her to go upstairs.

Unsteadily he said good-night to the boys. Then he forced himself to walk past the guest bedroom he'd assigned Chandra and down the hall to his own bedroom. He changed his mind and went to her room and opened the door. The trailing silk and lace nightgown and bed jacket he had picked up at a fancy shop on the way home lay across her empty bed, which was gilded by moonlight. He had hung several dresses in her closet and placed a shirt and a pair of jeans in her drawers, which she would no doubt discover in the morning.

He had made another stop before he'd come home—the drugstore, where he'd bought a package of condoms. Just in case he weakened and wasn't strong enough to resist her.

The drugstore cashier had recognized him and had given him an odd look as he'd rung up the purchase. Lucas had felt so hot under the collar he'd yanked his tie loose. The teenage cashier had chuckled and said, "Have a good one, Mr. Broderick."

Lucas went to his room. Slamming his briefcase on top of his desk beside his computer, he picked up the phone and hurriedly dialed his brother.

For once Pete answered on the first ring. Lucas could hear Sweet P. yelling in the background.

"Pete! Finally. I've been trying to get you all day. I've talked to your service, receptionists, machines—"

"Sorry. Two of my partners are on vacation, and the office and surgery schedule are jammed. How're the boys? They over their bout of flu yet?"

"You'd never guess they'd been sick."

"For a while there they really had me going with all those strange symptoms."

"You and me, brother."

"I couldn't figure out whether they were a pair of hypochondriacs or budding doctors," Pete said.

Lucas hesitated, not wanting to admit the truth. "I—I was wondering about that overdose patient with the head injuries who ran out on you at the ER."

Pete's voice tensed. "Now that's a strange situation."

"How?"

"Well, for one thing, we never found her. Then her records disappeared that same night. Everything, her chart, her medical history—it's even out of the computer. Which you, as a lawyer, would probably say is a lucky break for me because there's no record she was ever here. Which means I'm not liable. You know, even the red T-shirt we cut off her vanished." Pete hesitated. "Then yesterday, this guy called me about her and got really nasty."

"What?"

"He demanded to know the exact nature of her head injuries—how lucid she was, what she'd said, who she'd talked to. I told him several times that the doctor-patient relationship was privileged. He asked me if she'd talked to the police."

"So who was he?"

"The creep hung up before I could ask him. But you want to know something else really strange? His last question was about you. He asked me if you and I were related."

"And?"

"I told him it wasn't any of his business."

Worriedly, Lucas changed the subject and hung up a few minutes later. He opened his briefcase and took out the Moran will. A billion dollars was a hell of a motive.

But killing Chandra wouldn't change anything. The money would still go to the foundation.

Maybe somebody just wanted revenge.

Lucas found it difficult to concentrate as he read through the complicated document. He kept feeling alarmed that the caller had connected him to Pete.

Chandra was vulnerable and alone, perhaps running for her life. If some killer really was after her, Lucas should be comforting her and protecting her. Instead he had pulled that macho, I-have-to-have-my-space crap on her. Now he wanted her in this room where he could see her and know she was safe. He wanted to apologize. And yet he was afraid if he got near her again, he wouldn't be able to keep his hands off her.

No, this lonely hell was smarter than getting more deeply involved. He had to keep his distance—at least till he got some answers.

Still, it got harder and harder for Lucas to concentrate on the will. He couldn't stop wondering where she was or what she was doing or when she'd come upstairs to bed.

He thought of a dozen excuses to go downstairs—he was hungry for leftovers, he was thirsty for a soft drink, he needed to put the garbage out.

She'd already gotten the boys to put the garbage out.

He wanted only one thing—to be near her, to watch her, to listen to her. To get high on the buzz she gave him.

A dozen times he prowled across the room to the door and a dozen times he forced himself to return to his desk.

Finally he heard a faint sound on the bottom stair.
A light switch was flicked off. Next he heard hushed
footsteps in the hall and her soft voice as she said
good-night to the boys. Last of all came the sound of
her door easing open and softly closing.

She was next door—stripping, getting ready to
shower and go to bed.

The memory of her in his shower that had teased
and tortured him all day hit him again full force. He
remembered her breasts, the way the soapsuds had
clung to their hardened pink tips. He remembered her
bare skin had felt as soft as warm, living silk beneath
his hands. He remembered the hot taste of her sweet
mouth and the wondrous glory of her curved lips.
She'd been as light as a hummingbird when he'd
molded her to his body. He wanted to hold her again.
To kiss her again.

No. He wanted way more. He wanted her naked,
their bodies glued together, her legs and arms wrapped
around him, her mouth opening endlessly to his.

The mere memory of her coupled with his fantasy
made his blood run so hot, he felt drenched with desire. Finally he burst from his chair and paced restlessly to the door.

When he touched the doorknob, he felt it move ever
so slightly.

She was there.

He felt exactly as he had in the Moran foyer when
all the bitterness had left him and her gentler soul had
commingled with his.

Sensing her nearness, he stood stock-still, his heart
drumming. Had she felt his need for her and come to
him?

Desperately he swallowed and wiped his sweating brow with the back of his hand. She must not come in and find him lurking at the door ready to pounce on her like some sex-starved maniac. Then the doorknob turned, and he realized it was already too late.

When the door opened, he shoved it closed, leaning against it heavily to keep her and the desire he didn't want to feel for her at bay.

But she knocked gently.

He closed his eyes and clenched his fists as the rhythm of her knocks thudded inside him at the same mad pace as his heart.

He thought of the long, celibate months since Joan, when he'd buried himself in his work to avoid women. Was it any wonder that ever since that tantalizing episode in the shower, he couldn't stop thinking about Chandra? About her slender pale body or her dazzling sapphire eyes or her silken hair? He caught the scent from the roses on his bedside table. Even her scent was all around him. The entire house reeked of the damned flowers. The gardens outside brimmed with them. He had worn a rose she had given him to work.

Damn her! What was she trying to do to him?

Suddenly he couldn't stand knowing she was out there a second longer. Flinging the door open, he blocked her way into his bedroom like a hostile giant. With his legs thrust widely apart, his heart pounding faster, his whole body taut and perspiring, he demanded, "What do you want?"

He saw his own stark longing mirrored in her eyes. He saw her fear and sad confusion, too.

"I can't live like this. I want us to be friends," she whispered. "I want to make you happy."

Friends? Why did women always say crazy things like that? But the sound of her velvet-soft voice made his blood run like fire in his veins. "Impossible," he growled.

"Lucas," she began softly, "if my presence in your home is making things difficult for you, I'll leave."

"No!" God, no.

"But—"

Her face was deathly pale. Anxiety and exhaustion had darkened the bluish smudges beneath her eyes. She was barely out of the hospital. She didn't know who she was. She was fragile. What if the bastard who was trying to kill her got her?

She was wanted for murder. The cops would eat him alive. So would the media.

"And just where in the hell do you think you'd go?" he demanded roughly.

"I don't know."

"There. You see. You're safe here. That is *the* top priority. You have no choice but to stay."

"But if you don't want me here—"

"Did I say that?" he rasped. His heart thundered in agony.

"Then what is it? Talk to me."

He ran a shaky hand through his hair. "I can't. Not yet. This whole thing is—" He shrugged. "Hopeless. Just go back to bed."

She peered at him. "I'm begging you—talk to me. Why is that so hard?"

He caught the dizzying smell of her. He longed to touch the luscious skin of her bare arms again, and her throat, her cheek—knowing that every part of her would be as soft as roses. He longed to drag her into his arms and pull her close.

"Damn it, it just is."

Her sad eyes grew huge. "Lucas, I want to thank you for the clothes."

"You're welcome—so go," he ordered gruffly. The way she kept looking at him with her very soul lighting up her eyes got to him. "Look, you don't know who you are, and ever since I met you, I don't know who I am, either. This whole damn thing has me pretty rattled."

"Then you don't hate me?" she whispered, sounding pitiful and lost.

He fought the urge to grab her and comfort her and caress her. "Hate you?" He laughed mirthlessly even as her desperate eyes clung to his. "Good Lord, no. You want the truth, girl? I wish to hell I did hate you."

She kept her eyes fastened on the wall. Her voice was quiet. "I'm so sorry for causing you all this trouble."

"Just go to bed," he whispered raggedly. "Before I—"

Before I do something we might both regret in the morning.

"Okay." But her voice was unsteady, and she lingered a dangerous moment longer.

"What the hell are you waiting for?"

"For this." Impulsively she stretched onto her tiptoes and kissed his cheek. He shuddered at the unexpected fire of her lips. With her mouth on his and her breasts accidentally grazing his bare arms, his need for her racked through him.

Without thinking, his arms went around her and he dragged her to him and kissed her long and deeply, his lips playing greedily across hers, opening them.

Oh, God. She tasted like honey. Her sweetness invaded every pore of his body. She felt so good. His arms tightened around her.

Suddenly he pushed her away, his heart pounding. "Damn it. Go to bed, girl!"

Her eyes pleaded with him, invited him.

He felt almost a physical pain deep in his belly. He was about to seize her when she turned away shyly and ran.

The minute she was gone, he wanted her back.

He knotted his hands, scared he'd lose control again.

She wanted him, too, and turned, her blue eyes molten as she hesitated at her door.

She smiled and then grew very still.

He stared at her grimly, feeling awkward, unsure, as conflicting emotions surged inside him.

More than anything, he wanted to go after her.

"Good night," he croaked.

When her door shut behind her, he strode onto his balcony. His hands gripped the railing like talons as he leaned forward, staring sightlessly at the glistening bay and the waxing moon. Navy helicopters pulsed against the black sky as they buzzed across the bay on training missions. The waves sucked against wet sand. A bodyguard ambled lazily near the pool.

But all Lucas heard was *her* voice. All he saw was *her* face. Her body. All he tasted was her mouth. The memory of her shy smile haunted him, as did the wanton invitation in her eyes.

He wanted her badly.

He let the salt-scented breeze caress his perspiring body till it cooled him, and he gradually calmed down.

With iron control he undressed and crawled between the icy sheets of his bed.

But he couldn't sleep.

He lay in the dark as tense as a cat, wondering what he'd do if she screamed, as she'd done every night since she'd lived in his house. If he went to her room— If he so much as touched her velvet cheek, if he held her, he would have to taste her. Then he'd be lost for sure.

Lying in the dark, he thought of her lips and hair and breasts. He remembered her nipples growing hard when he'd stroked them.

God. He was driving himself crazy.

He jumped a foot when the telephone rang.

Usually he let the machine answer.

But he picked it up, glad for the distraction.

Six

Hesitantly Chandra leaned closer to the mirror, and as she did so, her image grew huge. Her lovely, enlarged face looked back at her sadly, questioning, as she raised a shaky fingertip and traced the shape of her mouth, still swollen from Lucas's kiss.

She lingered a second longer, and then, moistening her lips with her tongue, she pursed them and brushed them teasingly against the mirror.

The glass was cold.

Lucas's mouth had been hot and fierce and demanding, his arms crushing her.

So why had he rejected her?

Alone and miserable in her blue-tiled bathroom, her breath misting the glass, Chandra began to twist and untwist her yellow hair as she surveyed her pale features in the steam-clouded mirror, trying to find some fault in them. She rubbed the mirror with a towel.

A lone, glistening tear trickled from the corner of her eye down her pale cheek. She let her yellow hair fall to her shoulders. Always she was examining herself, trying new hairdos, new expressions, different postures, hoping for some tiny clue of recognition as to who she might be, hoping for a memory, a name, an image—anything other than those scary blue flashes.

Even before Lucas's rejection, she had felt erased. Formless. Shapeless. As if she was nobody.

But his rejection had left her too dispirited to even try to fight the amnesia. She was wondering why Lucas had returned from his office so dead-set against her. In that first instant when he'd seen her in his shower, his eyes had recognized her and adored her.

She couldn't be mistaken about that.

Yet after his passionate kisses and incredible kindness that morning, he had returned from his office determined to reject her.

Something had happened to him after he'd left her. Something that made him warier of her. And she hated that. For she wanted only to please him. All afternoon she had worked to make his homecoming special, to offer her thanks with a home-cooked meal and scented candles and friendship. But he had been hostile and rude and had gone out of his way to avoid her and reject her offerings.

Why?

If the argumentative exchanges with Lucas had left her feeling tired and very drained, that final rejection had finished her. She had been getting stronger every day. But now she felt almost as weak and depressed as she had the first day.

Wearily she leaned down and ran her bath. Then she pulled off her shirt and jeans and slipped into the tub. The warm water and foamy bubbles both soothed her and sapped what little remaining strength she had. She bathed quickly, then toweled herself off and put on the white diaphanous nightgown and the bed jacket Lucas had laid out on her bed.

She was so exhausted when she crawled into bed that she fell asleep the moment her head sank into the downy pillow, only to be jarred awake minutes later by the telephone on her nightstand. Impulsively she answered it at the exact moment Lucas did.

"Broderick here."

Without preliminaries a man said, "Damn it, Broderick. Have you found her?"

Chandra shot bolt upright in her bed, her knuckles whitening as she gripped the receiver. She knew without knowing *how* she knew that they were talking about her.

The other man's familiar voice made her shiver with horror.

"Damn it, no!" Lucas replied with a note of exasperation. "And don't call me at home. It's too dangerous."

Lucas's receiver clicked, but the other man stayed on the line a few tense seconds longer, breathing heavily, as if he sensed she was there. Then he hung up, and so did she.

Did Lucas know who she was? He had seemed familiar to her all along, and she'd registered that look of instant recognition when he'd first met her.

PLAY

SILHOUETTE'S

LUCKY HEARTS

GAME

AND YOU GET

- ★ FREE BOOKS
- ★ A FREE GIFT
- ★ AND MUCH MORE

TURN THE PAGE AND
DEAL YOURSELF IN ⟶

PLAY "LUCKY HEARTS" AND GET ...

★ **Exciting Silhouette Desire® novels—FREE**

★ **PLUS a lovely Austrian Crystal Necklace—FREE**

THEN CONTINUE YOUR LUCKY STREAK WITH A SWEETHEART OF A DEAL

1. Play Lucky Hearts as instructed on the opposite page.
2. Send back this card and you'll receive brand-new Silhouette Desire® novels. These books have a cover price of $3.99 each, but they are yours to keep absolutely free.
3. There's no catch. You're under no obligation to buy anything. We charge nothing — ZERO — for your first shipment. And you don't have to make any minimum number of purchases — not even one!
4. The fact is thousands of readers enjoy receiving books by mail from the Silhouette Reader Service. They like the convenience of home delivery…they like getting the best new novels months before they're available in stores…and they love our discount prices!
5. We hope that after receiving your free books you'll want to remain a subscriber. But the choice is yours — to continue or cancel, anytime at all! So why not take us up on our invitation, with no risk of any kind. You'll be glad you did!

NOT ACTUAL SIZE

You'll look like a million dollars when you wear this lovely necklace! Its cobra-link chain is a generous 18" long, and the multi-faceted Austrian crystal sparkles like a diamond!

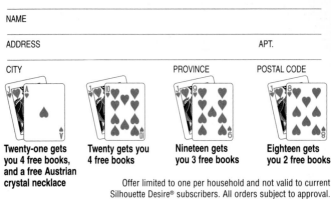

THE SILHOUETTE READER SERVICE™: HERE'S HOW IT WORKS

Accepting free books places you under no obligation to buy anything. You may keep the books and gift and return the shipping statement marked "cancel". If you do not cancel, about a month later we'll send you 6 additional novels, and bill you just $3.24 each plus 25¢ delivery and GST.* That's the complete price–and compared to cover prices of $3.99 each–quite a bargain! You may cancel at anytime, but if you choose to continue, every month we'll send you 6 more books, which you may either purchase at the discount price…or return at our expense and cancel your subscription.

*Terms and prices subject to change without notice.

Canadian residents will be charged applicable provincial taxes and GST.

SILHOUETTE READER SERVICE
PO BOX 609
FORT ERIE ON   L2A 9Z9

0195619199-L2A5X3-BR01

CDMA Member

If offer card is missing, write to: Silhouette Reader Service, P.O. Box 609, Fort Erie, Ontario L2A 5X3

MAIL▶POSTE
Canada Post Corporation/Société canadienne des postes
Postage paid   Port payé
If mailed in Canada   si posté au Canada
Business   Réponse
Reply   d'affaires
0195619199   01

Yet he'd sworn he'd never met her before.

Nothing made sense.

But then lies never did.

Could this mean his sons—

No. She would never believe Montague or Peppin were involved in anything other than helping her.

She got out of bed and went to her balcony. The lights in the aqua pool were on, so the rectangle gleamed like a jewel. The lawn was dark as it sloped down to the bay. In the moonlight, she saw two heavily built armed men, keeping to the shadows as they prowled the grounds. One of them stopped, his hand automatically going to his shoulder holster as he turned to stare at her.

And then she knew.

Her heart began to pound as she backed slowly into her bedroom and shut and locked the glass doors.

Lucas *had* lied.

Not only that. He had made her his prisoner.

Knowing she would never be able to sleep, she raced to his bedroom. She pushed the door open and rushed inside before she lost her nerve.

He flushed with guilt and angry surprise as he glanced at her from his desk and found her staring at him, wide-eyed, with her white gown floating around her hips because she had stopped so abruptly.

He wore pajama bottoms only. The sight of his dark bare chest with those odd scars and his muscular arms sent a shiver through her.

She seemed to have a similar effect on him. The moment he saw what she was wearing, his dark expression grew charged with desire. His heated gaze ran from her face down her body, which was clearly revealed by her nearly transparent nightgown. And as he looked at her, again she felt as if he were already her lover, as if he'd made love to her hundreds of times, as if they belonged together always.

She tried to remind herself how cold he'd been all evening. But he excited her. Underneath her doubt, some truer part of herself believed he was the one man who would never hurt her.

Vaguely she noted that his computer was on and that his briefcase lay open. Dozens of documents and files spilled from the briefcase all over his keyboard and cramped work space. When she walked toward him, her gown swirling seductively about her hips, he jammed several papers into his briefcase and snapped it shut before he jumped up. Suddenly she was curious not only about his mysterious caller and the strange men prowling outside, but about the contents of that briefcase.

"What were you working on?" she asked, surprising herself with the calm in her voice.

"Nothing." His voice was too crisp, too sharp. "I thought we already said good-night."

"Lucas, who are those armed men outside? Are you keeping me...prisoner?"

His turbulent gray eyes grew hard. "Damn it. I hired them to make sure no one bothers you while you're here."

"I've been here for days without guards."

"I hired them to protect you."

"Why now? I don't understand."

"Why now?" His eyes fastened on her face. "Because I didn't know about you till this morning. My kids rescued you out of a public hospital parking lot.

You were doped up and badly injured. You say somebody tried to kill you. You say you're scared they'll try again. And you ask me why? My reasons should be perfectly obvious. Anybody could have seen you get in my car. I don't know a damn thing about you or who might be after you. All I know is that you or my kids might be in danger.

"Also," he continued, "there's a guy making a name for himself killing Texas lawyers. In fact, he just blew an associate of mine away in Houston."

"I—I'm sorry about your friend, Lucas," she murmured.

"I received a death threat from the bastard—or from a crazy prankster pretending to be him—today."

She stared at him in mute horror.

Just for an instant his voice softened. "Now do you understand why I hired the bodyguards?"

The faint tilt of her head was barely perceptible.

"Good," he whispered. "I'm glad that's settled."

"Lucas, if you knew who I was . . . would you tell me?"

The merest fraction of a second passed before he answered. "Of course." His voice was smooth, easy, and yet there was another element in it. "Why do you ask?"

"Who called a while ago?"

This time there was no hesitation.

"It was a wrong number." His eyes burned into her, daring her to challenge the lie.

When she didn't he said, "Now would you go to bed?"

* * *

Later, in her bedroom, Chandra was dreaming she and Lucas were in a strange land and about to be married. Their silken costumes were exotic. A curtain of brightly colored beads hung in a doorway. All the women wore long gowns and veils. She wore a golden veil and golden bracelets, and Lucas was smiling at her, his gaze filled with warmth and love. But just as he was about to place the ring on her finger, his face changed and he was someone else. Someone with fierce black eyes and hate in his heart.

Then she was in another place and another time. It was almost as if she was another person. She was hiding from Lucas in a closet. He was in a room with tall ceilings. Dozens of vases and bowls held dying roses. People in black with long faces filed conspiratorially out of a library as Lucas dragged her out of a closet. The black-robed people nodded as he carried her away and locked her inside a dark, airless space. She began to scream as she realized he was going to bury her alive.

She cried Lucas's name again and again and woke to find herself in his beautifully appointed guest bedroom, its lilac colors bleached silver in the moonlight. She got up and, feeling cold, ran swiftly to open the doors. She stood in the draft of warm air, staring out at the bodyguard on the beach.

The night air was heavy with humidity. The tide had come in and the surf was rushing across the sand all the way to the rocks. She watched the water for a long time, but it did little to calm her. Her forehead and upper lip were beaded with perspiration as she shivered in terror from the residual horror of her nightmare.

"Hey, hey" came Lucas's gentle rasp from her doorway.

She had turned even before he spoke, because she had sensed he was there.

Their gazes met. In the silver light his harsh face was as unreadable as stone. Still, she felt that shock of recognition, and the electric excitement he aroused so easily rushed through her and mingled with her dread of him.

"It's only me," he murmured.

Again he was shirtless, and she stared at the brown chest covered with thick black hair. Still shaking with fright, she was struck by how strong and unyielding he was, and by how much she wanted to be held in his dangerous arms.

"Lucas—" Her mind swirled with all the fearful questions in her heart.

Again she felt that they had a past together, that they were more deeply involved than he was willing to let on.

"What's wrong?" he demanded.

"You were there," she whispered. "In my nightmare. You are one of them."

"No," he began hoarsely. "I'm not."

But she backed away from him, shivering, even as she longed to run to him and beg him to kiss her.

She forced herself to say, "You were plotting with them to kill me."

"No, oh, God," he whispered, reaching for her and cradling her body against his.

The sea breeze was ruffling her hair, sending long strands of the stuff against his cheek and throat. He smiled at her, his eyes kind as he stroked her cheek and smoothed her blowing hair. As he continued to hold her, she gradually relaxed. All night she had wanted this. Forever she had wanted it. If he knew who she was and wouldn't tell her, so be it. If she had to die, his arms were where she wanted to be.

With a helpless sigh she circled his neck with her trembling hands and whispered brokenly, "Not you. Please not you, too."

"I wasn't there."

She looked at him and saw that he burned with desire. The darker image of him looking hard and ruthless in that rose-filled foyer in her nightmare flashed into her mind.

"You were in a room filled with dying flowers."

He whitened, and she sensed there was more than an element of truth in her dream. And yet— *His eyes were kind.*

"Hold me," she whispered. "Just hold me."

At first his arms were gentle, but gradually they wound around her tightly until their bodies seemed to flow into one another and become one.

He had held her before. Many times.

She reached up and pressed a warm kiss against the hot skin of his neck. She felt his savage indrawn breath as male need raged through him. He buried his fevered lips in her hair with a hungry kiss that set her entire being aflame.

Without a word she began to explore his neck and throat with her mouth.

"Kiss me. Love me," she begged.

Unable to stand, they collapsed to the floor, their pulses beating together. She lay on the carpet, staring up at him as he silently tore off her clothes and then his own. When she was naked, his callused hands roamed from her breasts to her waist to her thighs, exploring, caressing, already knowing exactly what would most please her as if he was very experienced with her particular body. And she had that same instinctively accurate knowledge about him.

Soon she forgot everything except the pleasure of his delicately flicking tongue and his fingers moving urgently between her legs.

Her hands trailed over his hair-roughened chest, sensuously stroking ever lower down the length of his flat belly. She felt too aroused to ask him about the long scar on his torso. And as her fingers closed shamelessly around him, he swore, then groaned as he caught her waist and flipped her over onto her back.

Then he was on top of her, straddling her, his great dark body hot and hard and pulsating. His fingertips again stroked her inner thighs. She felt his thumbs skimming the satin folds between her legs, opening her like the petals of a rose.

As surprised as he, she cried out when he encountered the unexpected painful barrier.

"I'll stop," he offered hoarsely, desperately, "if you want me to."

"No." Her voice sounded as fractured as his. "Don't stop."

"But you're a virgin," he whispered. "I don't want to hurt you."

"It doesn't matter."

"To me it does." He pressed his lips to hers.

Arching her body to his, she cried out when he lowered his head to her breasts before sliding down the length of her until his open mouth was pressing against her most heated flesh. Then he began making love to her slowly while she moaned and twisted beneath him. Only when her knees clamped around his head did he quit kissing her and haul her underneath him again.

"Oh, God," he said, looking into her eyes. "You're beautiful."

She locked her arms around his neck. When he drove into her, her cry was filled with both rapture and pain. He whispered passionate endearments. After a while he slowly sank deeper. Then he began rocking harder and faster in a dreamlike, frictionless rhythm that was as old as time.

A rogue wave exploded on the beach below the white mansion, foam and spray shattering against the sand and racing up the beach to the bluff.

She felt carried away on a similar dark tide. The journey was like that great wave, swelling and swelling and then bursting into thousands of geysers before dying. And afterward, when she lay spent in a sated stupor of delirium and ecstasy, with his warm perspiring body sprawled heavily across hers, she clung weakly to his waist, tracing her trembling fingertips through his damp hair, never wanting him to let her go, never wanting the wondrous feelings she had for him to end.

When he recovered, he lifted her into his arms and carried her into his bedroom.

They did it in his marble shower because he had been fantasizing, ever since he'd met her there. This time he used a condom. With the warm water streaming down upon them, he braced her against the wall, entered her and then commanded her to wrap her legs tightly around him. His hands cupped her buttocks as he forcefully took her a second time.

"This is what I wanted the first instant I saw you," he growled.

Without a single reservation she urged him deeper. "Me, too."

Chandra felt as if she was in the middle of a swirling kaleidoscope of sunlight and brilliant hot colors as once again she was filled with him and felt the same building joy. And when it was over she was filled, as well, with the same unbearable and utterly illogical knowledge that tonight was not the first night they had made love.

But how could that be when she'd been a virgin?

Exhausted, they slept, their bodies intimately tangled beneath the sheets. In the middle of the night, he teased her awake by stroking her earlobe with his tongue, by trailing more kisses from her delicately arched feet up the curve of her thighs. But this time his lovemaking was softer and slower, and the pleasure she found in him indescribably spiritual. And again, he remembered to protect her.

When she awoke, a rosy light was sifting through his windows. How strange she felt, wrapped in his arms. She didn't care if she'd forgotten her life, as long as she'd found him. She felt so gloriously alive. Even though she was shamelessly naked beside him, she was not at all embarrassed.

She traced the gold design of his heavy cotton bedspread with a fingertip. Then she turned on her side and savored his nearness. His dark face seemed relaxed, almost content. With a sigh she melted against the heat of his long body.

She remembered how he had looked last night, with his silver eyes on fire for her, with his mouth heavy with sensuality. Slowly the bizarre realities of their situation returned. Her knowledge of him ran too deeply for them to have been strangers. And yet he swore he hadn't known her before.

He had posted armed bodyguards outside his house. He had talked cryptically about her to a man whose familiar voice terrified her.

Very carefully, so as not to awaken him, she untangled herself from his arms and legs and got out of bed. The room was shadowy as she glided to his closet and removed his terry robe. She had intended nothing more than to return to her room, but when she stumbled in the darkness, she bumped the corner of his black lacquered desk and saw his half-open briefcase. She stared at it, suddenly too curious to leave.

Her gaze flicked across the room when Lucas stirred. He had not opened his eyes.

Queasily she opened his briefcase.

And then she could only gape as she lifted a color blow-up of herself. In the picture her head lay across a stone block as she made a face at the camera.

Where? When?

Nothing clicked. Not even a blue flash. Absolutely nothing.

The photograph could have been that of a stranger. She lifted the paper under the photograph.

It was a pencil sketch. Again she recognized herself.

She dropped the photograph and the sketch as Lucas kicked his sheets off. She whirled and saw that he was watching her now from the shadows, his silver eyes predatory in the hot dawn light.

"What are you doing?"

She jumped at the steely sound of his low voice and slammed his briefcase. "I—I thought you were asleep," she whispered guiltily, her low voice betraying only the slightest trace of her fear.

"So you decided to spy."

"I was on my way to my room so the boys won't find us together."

"Leave my stuff alone and go," he commanded harshly, crawling out of bed.

"Who am I, Lucas?"

He hesitated and then said forcefully, "I don't know, damn it."

"Don't you?"

Before he could answer she turned and ran, too shaken by his dark look and rough tone to admit she'd seen the photograph of herself taken in another time and place and the sketch of herself as well.

Angrily he bunched the black embroidered spread at his waist and chased after her, catching her just inside her door.

"The boys," she whispered in a hurt, baffled voice. "I don't want them to hear us."

"I don't give a damn about the boys."

"You're angry, then?"

"No," he said softly, surprising her. "I'm sorry for the way I treated you. You caught me by surprise, that's all."

Very slowly he lifted her hands to his shoulders and then grasped her waist, drawing her stiff, reluctant body against his.

The bedspread fell to the floor.

She felt like she was melting in his heat.

"Marry me," he whispered.

"What?"

As always with her body plastered warmly against his, she found it impossible to think. But she knew that a proposal from him was no light, impulsive matter. And it scared her even more than the photograph.

"Forget your questions and doubts about me," he begged, "and I swear I'll forget mine about you."

"What if I can't?" she whispered, even though she was thrilled by his nearness as well as by the prospect of becoming his wife.

"We belong together. No matter what you've done or what I've done. No matter who you are. No matter how crazy and fast all this seems."

"I can't. Not till you tell me everything."

"Damn it, we met in my shower for the first time yesterday!"

"The truth is more complicated than that. My body held no secrets for you."

"Damn it. I can't explain my feelings. But you were a virgin. I swear I never made love to you before."

"Maybe we did everything else except for—" she blushed "—except the sex act itself."

"We didn't. I swear it. I never saw you. I never touched you. I never kissed you—before yesterday." He stared at her, his dark face intense and baffled. "But I can't blame you for thinking that. I don't have amnesia, but every time I'm with you I have the feeling I know you, too. You don't even have to talk, and I know what you're thinking and feeling. When you came to my door earlier, I knew you were out there even before I opened it. I'm confused, too. And a little scared. All I can think of to do is to give it time." A slow smile played around the corners of his mouth. "Maybe we should just enjoy it till we figure it out." He lowered his lips to hers.

"Are we going to make love again?"

His voice grew husky. "Is that an invitation?"

When she was silent, he lifted her into his arms and carried her inside, kicking the door shut behind them.

He wasn't telling her everything.

But his body radiated heat and his touch was tender as he laid her beneath him on the bed.

She didn't know whether his kisses were taking her to heaven or hell. His hard body rasped silently against her soft breasts and stomach and thighs. His mouth and hands explored her hungrily, leaving no part of her unclaimed. When he pushed her legs apart and drove inside her, she cried out because the indescribable pleasure he gave her made her whole.

In that final heated moment of melting release, she didn't care who he was. Or who she was.

Or even if he was her worst enemy.

She put a hand on either side of his hot cheeks, and with utmost deliberation, kissed him on the mouth.

The act was a pledge.

No matter who he was, she belonged to him.

She always had and she always would.

Seven

Billion-Dollar Moran Heiress Wanted For Murder.

The two-inch-high newspaper headline slammed into Lucas's gut as hard as a balled fist.

If Chandra read that headline, she might get her memory back in a hell of a hurry. But what would such an unpleasant shock do to her?

His hand jerked, causing him to splash hot coffee all over himself. On the front page was a full-color photograph of Chandra and a lurid shot of the coffin that contained what was left of Miguel Santos. There was a small story about Gertrude Moran's new will and rumors that the notorious Lucas Broderick had been hired by the family to break the will.

Damn.

A feeling of profound dread filled Lucas.

Chandra had looked so pale and fragile this morning when he'd left her asleep in her bed. Too fragile to deal with this.

Any minute she'd be down for breakfast. If some slimy bastard really was after her, he could have leaked the stories to the press to flush her out. If she turned herself in to the law and didn't get her memory back, the cops would crucify her.

Lucas decided he couldn't let her see this yet. She didn't need any additional trauma. But that wasn't what scared him the most. To tell her the truth now might be a further risk to her life. If she felt compelled to talk to the cops or to reporters, the killer would know exactly where she was.

Grabbing a towel, Lucas sopped up the spilled coffee and then raced to the den, where he punched his television remote. News stories about the Moran scandal blared from every channel. One showed Santos's weeping widow in a black shawl with her five weeping children slumped together on rickety folding chairs in a small adobe chapel for the funeral service. Another showed shots of officers pulling sacks of drugs out of the burned van. In still another a cop was saying that they had the red T-shirt Chandra was last seen wearing, and that Santos's blood was all over it. There was only one positive story. It was about Casas de Cristo and the houses Chandra had built for barrio families. Lucas listened closely to the interviews with Mexican officials and several poor families who touchingly defended her, saying that Chandra could not possibly be involved in anything illegal.

When his phone rang, Lucas grabbed it, and a drunken Stinky roared obscenities into his ear.

"I'm as upset about this as you are, Brown. But if you call me at home again, we're through." Lucas slammed the phone down.

The heat to solve the mystery was on. Only it was even worse than Stinky had predicted. The press was going to town with the scandal. Chandra was so hot, she had even upstaged the serial killer who'd threatened Lucas.

Suddenly Lucas heard his boys' stampeding footsteps and rough shouts as they raced downstairs. As he switched off the television set, Montague and Peppin burst in upon him.

"We know who she is, Dad," Peppin exclaimed in a breathless rush. "Her name's Bethany Ann Moran and she's real real rich and—"

"I know," Lucas said quietly.

"They're framing her, Dad!" This from Montague. "She didn't kill anybody. We gotta make the cops see that."

"Look, guys, I've been thinking. Maybe it's not such a hot idea to turn her over to the cops—I mean, right now, when some goon is after her and before she gets her memory back. We need to be able to prove she's innocent. Otherwise the cops might slap her in jail. It's a good idea to come clean, but we can always do it later. I want you to get every television set and radio out of the house and put them in my car."

"But, Dad, maybe if we tell her who she is, she'll get her memory back. Maybe she can tell the cops exactly what happened. Who the real killer is. And then she could live here always."

"No, dumbo. She's rich. Do you think she'd still want to stay with us after she found that out? She'd leave."

Both boys grew silent at that possibility.

"I don't think we should decide anything without medical advice," Lucas said. "I'm driving her to San Antonio to see Pete today. And I'm not even going to try to find a sitter for you guys—so I want you two to come straight home from school and intercept and destroy every newspaper or magazine that carries this story."

"Dad, how come you're trying to help her when those guys on TV say you've been hired to break the Moran will—"

"Shut up, Peppin. We gotta start uplugging stuff fast," Monty ordered tersely. "Dad's on her side the same as we are."

"Holy cow! She's rich and the bad guys are after her. Maybe after us, too. This is way better than a movie," Peppin crawed. "I'm gonna get my baseball bat out of my closet and hide it under my pillow along with my knife."

"What good will that do?"

"Stupid! What if *he* gets in here?"

"Boys, not now."

Electrified into action that appealed to them immensely, they raced up and down the stairs, whispering and arguing about strategies a mile a minute while they filled Lucas's trunk and back seat with every electronic gadget in the house.

Lucas went to Chandra's bedroom to distract her. When he entered the lilac room, Chandra was dressed in the new yellow dress with the tight bodice and full skirt he'd bought her. She was leaning across her bed, so that he got a marvelous view of her slim waist, shapely hips and long legs as she straightened the spread.

He closed the door with a click, and she stopped tucking the pillow under the lilac silk spread and smiled spontaneously.

Enraptured, he could only stare at her speechlessly.

"So, there you are," she said, rushing to him. "I just couldn't seem to wake up after—"

A wanton image rose in both their minds of their bodies writhing together. Blushing, she tossed her mane of hair and laughed. Her blue eyes glowed. The shadows beneath them were very faint.

"You look wonderful in that dress."

"Thank you. You have excellent taste."

"Not usually."

She could not seem to stop looking at him any more than he could stop looking at her. Again he was stunned that the foundations of his life had shifted so swiftly and so irrevocably.

"I was afraid you might have already gone to your office," she said hesitantly.

"Without kissing you goodbye?" he murmured.

As she stretched on her tiptoes to offer him her lips, he caught her fiercely against his immense frame and held her for an endless moment. And as he did, a lifetime of bitter emotion flowed out of him.

He had known her a mere twenty-four hours, and already she was the single thread of his life, the one thing that, if severed, would destroy everything. No matter what he had to do, no matter what lie he had to tell or what secret he had to keep, he couldn't lose her.

"I am going downtown, but not for long," he murmured. "I've decided to spend as much time as I can with you—until I'm sure you're completely recovered."

"But, Lucas, that's not necessary. The last thing I want is to be a burden to you."

"You're not. I'm linked by modem, telephone and fax to my office. I can work here almost as easily as there. But I'm taking off today to drive you to San Antonio."

"Why?"

"My brother is a doctor. I want him to check you and to make sure that you're really okay."

"That's not necessary."

"Just say you'll go."

"But—"

"I thought you wanted to make me happy."

"I do."

"So, will you go?"

"Yes. Yes. Yes."

He grinned at her. "Why can't you say that when I ask you to marry me?"

"I will . . . soon. I'm sure of it. Only—"

Her voice trailed off. Her blue eyes were troubled, her white face fragile.

Lucas's heart filled with panic. He was used to getting what he wanted when he wanted it. If she didn't marry him now, maybe she never would.

He analyzed the situation with his cold lawyer's intelligence that not even the fire of his new passion could altogether extinguish. Once she knew who she was and who he was, once the media and the police and her family started in on her, anything could happen.

He needed time to win her.

Time to figure this mess out.

And he was running out of time.

Lucas strode hurriedly across the plush Oriental rugs and unlocked the cabinet that contained his private fax machine. There were two curled pieces of shiny paper in the tray. He picked them up and began to read.

TIGER ONE SECURITY AGENCY
1414 Shoreline Boulevard
Corpus Christi, Texas

Fax to: Lucas Broderick
Fax from: Tiger Security

Dear Lucas:

Subject held in high esteem in northern Mexico by Rafe and Cathy Steele.

The Steeles temporarily in charge of Casas de Cristo since subject's disappearance. Steele very suspicious and belligerent to our questions.

Subject regarded highly by her benefactors and employees. Friends swear drugs were planted in her houses.

Truck driver who picked subject up on highway night van burned has positively identified her photograph.

Unable to contact witness who says subject was driving burned vehicle.

Subject's fingerprints all over the unregistered

Colt .45 police claim killed Santos.

Police determined to build a case against subject.

Media camped outside Moran ranch.

Holly Moran pretended to be reluctant about giving evidence, but she told police that Chandra had said she was on her way to ranch. She also gave damning evidence about subject's mental state.

Everybody at ranch denies seeing subject or van at the ranch the day of memorial service.

Henry Moran illegally sold guns to Central American freedom fighters.

Stinky Brown's parents died in bizarre boating accident. Stinky did jail time in the eighties for beating up and nearly killing a rich debutante who jilted him right before he dated Chandra.

Unable to confirm Brown's claim that his brother Hal has gone east to visit relatives.

No criminal record on any of the Morans or Hal Brown.

More details to follow.

> Sincerely,
> Tom Robard

The second fax was a long list of Chandra's unsavory boyfriends.

Lucas wadded it up and burned it in his ashtray.

As he watched the names go up in flames, he felt a raging jealousy. Until he remembered that she'd been a virgin.

Feeling calmer, Lucas locked Robard's fax in a drawer filled with other confidential reports in the same cabinet that contained his private fax machine.

Lucas felt more restless and dissatisfied than ever. Other than her friends' belief in Chandra, there was nothing to exonerate her.

Damn it. She was innocent.

But he had to prove it.

Lucas sat down at his desk and dialed Stinky.

"Have you found her?" Stinky's slurred voice was like ice.

"No."

"Then you're fired, counselor."

Both men slammed down their phones.

Lucas sighed ruefully. If only the rest of this mess could be solved so easily.

His intercom buzzed, and Lula's brisk voice informed him that a police detective, a Lieutenant Sheldon, was outside.

"And there's a reporter from the *Caller* who wants to talk to you when the lieutenant is finished."

Black-gloved hands clenched the steering wheel. "Gotcha!" A poisonous hammering began inside the watcher's skull.

From the driver's seat of a nondescript gray car that was parked four houses down from Lucas's opulent white wall, the watcher smiled as Lucas Broderick's Lincoln swept out into the bustle of traffic on Ocean Drive.

The watcher's eyes went glassy with delight when they fastened on the girl in her late twenties with the showy blond hair. *Beth!*

Broderick's arm was draped over the seat, his hand casually resting on her bare shoulder. She was thinner, but she looked almost well again. Maybe not completely. But no longer was she the battered, bleeding, vacant-eyed zombie who had emerged from the burning van and dashed suicidally in front of that truck.

She leaned closer to Broderick, and the watcher realized she was in love.

Big damn surprise.

So, the sickening hunch had been dead on the money. All the waiting and careful plotting worth it.

Broderick was a liar and a thief and a gold digger. He'd had her the whole damn time.

When the bastard had seen a way to do better than his forty-percent fee, he'd sure as hell gone for it.

Broderick had lied to the family as well as to all the authorities.

Which meant the bastard had to die, too.

The beast inside the watcher smiled grimly.

The gray car slid into traffic and, lagging a safe distance, followed the Lincoln all the way to San Antonio.

All the way to Dr. Pete Broderick's discreet brick mansion in the woody hills on the fashionable northwest side of San Antonio.

Bastards. All of them.

But they'd be sorry.

The beast was free and on the rampage.

At long last.

For Lucas the next few days were wonderful and terrible and desperately crucial. He had to win Chandra so completely that when she knew the truth, she would forgive him everything. At the same time he had to protect her and solve the mystery.

Somehow Lucas had convinced the police and the press he knew next to nothing about the Moran case, and they turned their attentions elsewhere.

Lucas had warned Pete not to reveal anything he knew about Chandra's true identity before he'd taken her to San Antonio. Pete said that Chandra's injuries hadn't been as severe as the emergency room doctors had led him to believe. He also confirmed her belief that she couldn't have done better with teams of surgeons and nurses caring for her. But when Pete got Lucas alone, he said Lucas was correct to fear her mental state was still very fragile, that she needed to be nurtured and protected and that she should not be told who she was and especially not that she was wanted for murder until she was a good bit stronger.

"She is blocking the truth because it's too horrible to accept."

"So, when can I tell her?" Lucas had demanded tensely.

"Give her a week. Till Friday, at the very earliest. Say, what is she to you anyway?" Pete smiled. "I've never seen you so—"

Lucas frowned, unwilling to say. "She's . . . good with the boys."

"I'll bet!" Pete flashed him a grin. "The family's going to love her."

"Oh, yeah. For sure. She'll fit right in. Another missionary. Just what we need."

"She's just what *you* need. And you know it."

Pete changed her medicine and gave Lucas a sheet of instructions and joked that Peppin and Montague might indeed make good doctors. When Lucas and Chandra drove away from his house with Pete's glowing report, Lucas's spirit rocketed sky-high. He hugged her close for a very long time, feeling immensely relieved that she was over the worst of her injuries and that her amnesia wouldn't be permanent. In fact, he was so thrilled by the prognosis that he decided to celebrate. For the next few hours he forced himself to set aside his fears for her and the sensation that danger was thickening all around them, and he simply enjoyed being with her.

Lucas found an out-of-the-way restaurant and ordered a seafood dinner to go. Then he took her to a state park in the hill country where the warm air was sweet with the scent of cedar and a clear green river ran between tall limestone cliffs. They ate beneath the spreading branches of a live oak tree. Then they slow-danced beside his car to the music from a tape in the car player. They drove home in the star-spangled darkness, roaring along the straight interstate with the windows of the Lincoln partially down so that wisps of her hair blew against his cheek. He drove at a speed that made his blood rush with excitement, or maybe it wasn't the speed that made his blood heat but the fact that she was nestled in his arms.

It was two in the morning when the big car nosed its way through the white walls and up the drive to his house. They went inside and made sure the boys were safely asleep. Then he took her down to the beach where they walked hand in hand, barefoot along the water's edge.

He felt like he was in a dream as he led her running through the warm salt water and then across the sand up to the doors to the tunnel in the bluff.

He started to unlock the heavy steel doors, but she turned white and said no, that she wanted to take the path up the cliff to the house.

"But this is the shortcut," he whispered, "and soon it'll be sealed up for good."

She trembled and forced herself to take slow deep breaths. "The sooner the better. The very idea of it gives me the creeps."

He grinned. "You and my Realtor. I need to call a contractor."

She smiled at him. Then she turned and raced up the cliff path. He dropped the lock, and it banged against the metal door as he chased after her.

Before they let themselves in through the patio doors that opened onto the deck, he sprayed the sand off their feet and ankles with the hose. Together they raced along the dimly lit corridors and stairways to his room, where they closed the door and she lit candles. Then they fell upon his bed and made love to each other greedily, desperately, as if they could never get enough of each other.

And this time he didn't practice safe sex because he selfishly knew that he wanted a baby from her. She was wonderful with his boys. And the image of her holding a baby, his baby, maybe a little girl with blue eyes and golden hair like hers, branded itself into his soul.

But it wasn't only the child he wanted. It was Chandra who was the ultimate prize. She had to be his, and he knew if he got her pregnant that would be still another bond that might make her want to stay with him forever.

Even in love that ruthless quality in his nature that had driven him to excel in law drove him to conquer, obtain, acquire whatever he wanted. There was an insatiable, selfish completeness about his feelings for her that made him know he *had* to win her.

For better or for worse, he was head over heels in love with her. He *had* to marry her.

But when he told her so and asked her to marry him again, she held him very close and kissed him. Then she said no.

Almost imperceptibly the tensions between Lucas and Chandra built during that week. The police talked to him again, as did the press. He told the reporters that he was no longer representing the Morans.

Determined to be with Chandra every possible minute, Lucas worked at home as much as he could. But spending more time with her taught him how vastly different were their personalities and characters. She was cut of finer, nobler cloth than the base stuff he was made of.

After reading dozens of Robard's reports about her missionary work, Lucas couldn't help but compare her inner purity to his own selfishness. He was unworthy, shallow, materialistic. He had lived solely for himself before he met her, seizing what he wanted with no thought of the consequences to others. He had charged to the max for his services, his only restraints being—can I get away with it without breaking the law?

Ruthlessly he had gone after only the cases that could make him rich or famous. He had sacrificed idealism at the twin altar of his ego and ambition. He had sacrificed friendships, his first marriage, his integrity, even his sons.

And though his love for Chandra had changed him to some degree, he knew that he would never be a white knight. Even though he felt ashamed and was determined to change, he could not totally remake himself. Thus he, who had always been so brashly self-confident, was afraid that she wouldn't love him when she really knew him.

He forced himself to back out of juicy cases, but signed on to defend a group of immigrants whose landlords refused to provide indoor plumbing.

Less than pleased with the new Lucas Broderick, his law partners began grilling him about some of his decisions. They were furious that he'd lost the Moran case. He told them he'd quit the firm and go out on his own if they didn't let him do as he pleased.

More than anything, he was working to find some shred of evidence to prove Chandra's innocence. Her memory didn't return, but she was so intuitive about him that she sensed the darkening in his mood every time he returned from his office knowing Robard had found nothing to clear her, only more that incriminated her.

The media coverage grew more shocking by the day, the rumors about her more vicious. The federal government decided to investigate her. What disturbed Lucas most was that the most damning stories about Chandra's supposedly shady operation in Mexico were his own idea. Only he hadn't ordered his men to spread those rumors. Someone who had been in the Moran library had.

But who?

According to Robard, every single person in that library had an airtight alibi the night of Santos's murder.

Lucas used some of his time at home to take care of mundane chores around the house that he never had time for. He met with the contractor and set Saturday as the day to seal the tunnel.

The images in Chandra's nightmares were becoming clearer. The memory of Lucas in a room with gilt furniture and dying roses was becoming sharper. She said she remembered being locked in a dark room and repeatedly drugged with syringes. She remembered a man with black eyes.

Practically all the Morans and everybody on the ranch had black eyes. Stinky's were the darkest. But Stinky and Holly had been entertaining mourners at the ranch the entire evening of the murder. So had Hal. At least according to Stinky.

Every night, after one of Chandra's nightmares, Lucas would hold her close and comfort her until her face lost its chalky pallor and she could breathe and talk normally. Last night she had dreamed she'd crawled out of a van right before it caught fire.

Every day that passed, his tensions and fears coiled around Lucas more tightly. He felt trapped in a spider's web.

Only he couldn't see the spider.

Their quarrel started with a phone call.

Lucas and the boys were out by the pool, so Chandra, who had just gotten up from her afternoon nap, answered the phone. When Lucas came running inside to catch it, he found her leaning against the kitchen counter looking numb, her white face as frozen as if she'd just awakened from a nightmare.

"Who is it?"

"I don't know. He won't say anything."

Lucas tore the phone from her. "Who the hell is this?"

The line was dead.

Lucas slammed the phone down. "How many times do I have to tell you not to answer the damn phone?"

"Well, excuse me for living," she whispered tightly, rushing past him up the stairs. "I was tired. I didn't think."

He raced after her, feeling fury, remorse, love—the whole impossible gamut.

"I want you to tell me what is going on," she demanded when he followed her inside her bedroom.

"No. I need you to trust me."

She sat in front of her bureau and stared anxiously at her reflection in the mirror. With a tentative fingertip she pushed her hair and touched the fading zipperlike scar at her hairline. The scratches on her cheek were almost gone. She was growing stronger by the day. She spent less and less time taking naps.

"Trust you? There's nothing I want more. But that's very hard when I have no memory. I feel so empty and yet I keep having these terrible flashbacks. I love you and yet I know that you're keeping secrets from me."

"I told you. Pete said you need a week or so more to recover—"

She whirled. "I'm sick and tired of being treated like a baby."

"You nearly died. You need to get well. I'll tell you everything Friday."

"Friday? That's three whole days away. I don't know if I can wait."

Gently he tucked a stray strand of gold behind her ear. "Friday, I swear," he pleaded softly. "Maybe it won't even be that long. Maybe you'll get your memory back before then. Maybe the guys who are after you will make a wrong move."

"But this waiting, feeling like we're being stalked is hell. If I knew everything you know, maybe I could help you."

"Maybe. But right now your most important job is to rest and get well. If I don't have all the answers by Friday, I don't see that we have any choice but to do as you ask. Trust me . . . just a little longer."

She stared at him gloomily, moodily—hesitating.

"I know it's hard," he said reaching for her.

"Do you? You're always so in control!" She spun away from him. "I can't stand the way I feel—like we're living under siege."

"Look, some bastard tried to kill you. I'm afraid he'll try again."

"Why can't I at least watch television? Or listen to the radio?"

He shifted slightly, so that even if she wouldn't let him touch her, he was near enough to feel the warmth of her body.

"Because it might upset you too much. We agreed . . . Friday. If you don't get your memory back or I don't solve this thing, I'll do it your way."

Again she moved away from him. "I—I feel so trapped and isolated—so afraid."

"That's why I stay home as much as I can."

Her wide luminous eyes said, *But I'm afraid of you, too.* Aloud she whispered, "Lucas, you're in all my nightmares now, and you're always against me."

"No! I'm on your side. I swear it. You belong to me. I belong to you. I love you. I would lay down my life for you."

She didn't answer.

He got down on his knees in a posture of supplication. "Look into my eyes. What do you see?"

She knelt, too, and cupped his jaw with her fingertips. As she stared at him, the flame in her eyes lit an answering spark of emotion inside him.

"I do see love. Pure love," she whispered at last, "but I'm not sure if I can trust that."

"What else is there to believe in? What else is worth dying for?"

The late-afternoon sunlight was streaming through the windows. She looked wan and very vulnerable and so tired he could almost feel her exhaustion. He felt the same ache he always felt when he watched her sleep in the afternoons or at night when he comforted her after one of her nightmares.

Her luminous blue eyes continued to search his, distrusting him even though he knew she saw all the way into his heart. "I would die for you, too," she said.

He nodded, although he wasn't satisfied, and pressed his lips together tightly. "Let's hope it doesn't come to that."

"Lucas, last night I dreamed about that man's gray face again. It caught fire. His skin melted. But I saw a mustache this time, and the color of his dead eyes. They're brown—almost black. Who is he? Why does he haunt me? Why do I feel so guilty every time I see him staring at me with open-eyed horror?"

Santos.

Oh, God.

Tell her.

Lucas's hand closed around hers and gave it a nervous squeeze. "Friday."

Eight

"Gotcha!"

The good-for-nothing lardy bodyguard never saw the horseshoe aimed at the back of his skull.

One minute the oaf was staring at the placid brown bay. The next he was crumpling heavily forward into the grass. Then the bloody horseshoe was picked up by a black-gloved hand and pitched onto the grass with the others. Slowly the watcher leaned down and grabbed the guard's ankles. The limp body was dragged, feet first, head bouncing along the stone path past the rose garden and into the garage. The doors were opened and the inert body was dragged inside the tunnel.

The beast felt excited as he heaved the bloated guard beside the other unconscious guard, who was gagged and bound. This was almost as good as shooting Santos and setting his body on fire.

Murder was the best of all highs.

Especially when it meant you didn't have to share what was rightfully yours with someone you hated.

The beast, who had stalked Lucas Broderick and Chandra Moran for the past week, should know. For the beast, the real person, had killed four times. And loved it.

The first murder had been the hardest.

The second had been Gertrude Moran.

The third—Miguel Santos.

The fourth had been that other self that had dared to inhabit the same body and had tried to cage the beast.

The false person had been pleasant and likable and had had lots of false friends. The false person had not cared that the beast seethed with rage and hurt and hatred every time the false person was nice to the false friends.

But the beast had vanquished the false person forever. There would be no more smiles that made the shared lips feel stiff or twitchy, no more lies that nauseated the real person.

While he thought, the beast methodically stripped the bodyguard and tied and gagged him. Next the beast put on the bulky uniform, the badge, the gun.

Then the beast felt powerful. All powerful—like a god.

The beast locked the brass padlock to the tunnel and strutted out of the garage into the brilliant, late-afternoon sunshine.

The oversize uniform was hot and scratchy.

So the hell what?

It would be dark soon, and cooler.

From the edge of the lawn, standing in a thicket of mesquite and tallow trees, the beast watched Lucas's Lincoln sweep into the drive. The black eyes narrowed as Lucas got out of the car with an armload of roses. The eyes became slits when Beth rushed out of the house and laughingly blushed as she took them. Her showy golden hair swirled about her shoulders as the lying bastard lifted her and made love to her first with his gaze and then with his lips.

Damn the bitch.

How the hell had she gotten out of that van? She should have fried.

Anger suffused every cell. Damn the lying betraying bastard lawyer for hiding her.

Obscene gurgling sounds came from the back of the beast's throat as Beth kissed Broderick deeply and passionately.

Fingers itched along the smooth trigger.

A silent voice cautioned, "*Wait till it's time.*"

A station wagon filled with six or seven boys rolled up. Both back doors were kicked open. Broderick's two brats spilled out of the house and raced toward the wagon.

After a parental lecture from Broderick and hugs from Beth, the little devils got in the wagon with their duffel bags to be driven away.

But the nosy kid with the ponytail lowered his silver sunglasses and stared long and hard at the beast until the wagon rolled out of the drive.

Melting into each others' arms, Beth and Lucas obviously thought they had the house to themselves and were looking forward to a romantic evening.

Little did they know.

The beast couldn't wait to sneak up on them and whisper, "Gotcha!"

Nine

Lucas sped home by way of Ocean Drive. There was a sailboard regatta on the bay. Not that he paid the slightest attention to the brightly colored sails rounding the final mark before skimming downwind toward the finish line as gracefully as butterflies. Nor did he note the landscaped mansions with their sculptured green lawns, palm trees, scarlet bougainvillea and pink oleander.

The traffic was heavy. But he didn't pay much attention to the steady stream of red taillights in front of him.

His mind was on Chandra.

It was Friday. Chandra had given Lucas till midnight to level with her. Even though he'd sworn he'd tell her everything, the week had gotten no better as it had worn on. If anything, the tension between Chandra and him had worsened. She had grown stronger and more restless by the day. She never napped now, and had more time to fret. She said she felt like a prisoner, that the suspense of not knowing her identity was killing her. Lucas had repeated Pete's advice so many times it had become a refrain. "Baby, Pete says it'll be better if you recover your memory on your own."

"I just keep thinking you'd tell me unless I—I'm some terrible sort of person—"

"It's complicated. You're not a terrible person."

"Then why are you so afraid to tell me?"

He always changed the subject at that point.

Lucas felt worried as he drove up to his house. Neither he nor Robard was a damn bit closer to solving the mystery of Miguel Santos's murder or to proving Chandra's innocence. And Lucas, who had built and won so many cases, Lucas who had written so many closing arguments to convince juries, couldn't seem to figure out the right words or the right way to tell Chandra something as straightforward as the simple truth.

Your family hired me to break the Moran will and defame you. I was tempted. God, how I was tempted. Until I found out who you were. Oh, and, by the way, you're wanted for murder, and the media are roasting you alive. They're saying you're a liar and a thief and that you've been taking bribes down in Mexico. They say you've run drugs. And, oh, I gave the lying bastard who's spreading this garbage the idea to slander you.

Lucas hadn't lived like a saint. Making her believe in his innocence and his love for her wouldn't be easy.

He had been boxed into tougher corners than this one.

But he had to win this one.

She'd been in his home less than three weeks, but already he depended on her quiet efficiency around the house. Already he delighted in the wonderful meals she took such pains to prepare for him. Already he admired her wonderful rapport with his sons and loved the way she made it possible for him to enjoy them, too. Peppin had even been bringing home a few As on his report card.

Most of all, of course, Lucas simply wanted Chandra for himself. In his bed. By his side. All the time. He wanted to bask in the loving glow he felt whenever he was around her. Forever. She made him happy. She made even the duller moments in his life meaningful and joyful. Just knowing she was in his house made the darkness lift from his soul.

Romantic gestures were alien to him.

But he'd bought flowers for this occasion. And a good sparkling California wine from a château he'd once visited in Sonoma.

Before he told her the truth, he wanted to set the mood.

The boys were scheduled to go on a beach camp out at a neighbor's house with several friends. He and Chandra would have the house to themselves.

Lucas had bought a steak for himself as well as roses. And lots of vegetables, everything from zucchini to spinach.

After dinner he planned to woo her and make love to her.

Afterward he would tell her. Maybe she'd even let him put it off until the morning.

And just in case she understood and forgave him, he had bought an engagement ring.

He would broach the shocking truth with infinite gentleness and patience. He would go down on his knees when he confessed he had been hired to steal her inheritance and defame her. He would tell her about the incident in the foyer, when he hadn't even seen her but had been so shaken by her presence. About all the dreams he'd had before he'd met her, especially the nightmare he'd had the night she'd been injured.

Somehow he had to make her believe what he himself did not understand—that the two of them had a special bond that went far beyond the ordinary.

He had to make her see that even though he had considered the Moran case and worked for the Morans briefly, he had never deliberately done anything to hurt her.

Except to show some slimy bastard how to slur her good name and thereby ruin her reputation.

He only hoped that the truth would change things for the better between Chandra and himself, instead of for the worse.

Tonight. Tomorrow at the latest. No matter what, he would tell her the whole, unvarnished truth. Who she was. Who he was. And then he'd show her the newspapers that he'd been keeping in his trunk and beg her to forgive him.

They would face this thing together.

As he got out of the Lincoln he noted the bodyguard in a baggy uniform, slouching against a palm at the far edge of his property.

A new man. That was odd. Lucas thought he knew all Robard's men.

The guard sensed his interest, and when Lucas waved to him, the guy's hand went to his gun for a second before he lifted his hand and waved back. Then he skulked behind the palm tree.

Damned odd fellow. Gave off negative vibes. Worth investigating.

Lucas was about to go over and introduce himself when Chandra came running out of the house to greet him.

She hesitated on the last step, and he saw the fear and uncertainty in her eyes as well as the radiance of her love.

She was just as afraid of tonight as he was.

Concerned only for her, he forgot the bodyguard. This thing was hard on her. She'd been through a lot. *But maybe not the worst of it.*

She was wearing the aqua dress with tiny pearl buttons down the front he had bought for her the first day. Strands of fine gold hair were blowing in the faint breeze. There was a private smile, just for him, on her lips.

He grinned and held up the roses. And felt a little foolish. Four dozen red, pink, white and yellow blossoms spilled from his arms.

When she flashed him an even brighter smile and began to blush, walking shyly toward him, his chest swelled with the passionate emotion he felt for her, which was growing more incredibly potent with the passing of every day.

Her eyes were ablaze when he gently gave her the flowers.

Their fingertips brushed, and as always there was magic and warmth even in her lightest touch.

Then she buried her nose in the fragrant petals and said softly, ''I love roses. Why do you suppose I love them so much?'' She looked at him. ''But not nearly as much as I love you. Now why do I feel—'' Her blue eyes flashed and she broke off shyly.

Her face was flushed. Her entire being seemed aglow. And her warmth filled him.

Nobody had ever cared about him as she did. Not when he was a child. Not when he was a man. He had been lonely all his life.

Till her.

He had had success—wealth, fame. Everything and nothing—till her.

He hadn't believed in love.

Because he hadn't had the slightest idea what love was.

Till he'd stepped into his shower and her dazzling blue eyes had seared his soul the same way they were doing now.

For far too long he had wanted all the wrong things for all the wrong reasons—to make up for the emptiness inside him.

But they never had.

She alone could make him happy.

He was too old not to know that this sort of feeling wouldn't come twice in his lifetime.

He had to make her stay with him forever.

Lucas had wanted the evening to be perfect, and it was. She seemed to understand the ephemeral quality of everything they did together, that when she knew the truth, everything they had come to count on and cherish might be lost.

So for this brief shimmering space of time, they both wanted nothing except each other.

The sky darkened to opalescent purples and lavenders and indigos. Lucas and Chandra were easier with each other than they had been all week, their words and glances accompanied by frequent quiet laughter.

He warmed dinner and then they swam while the food was heating up. She lay in a lounge chair, content to admire his long brown body sliding through the water. The blue heron she sometimes fed on the patio flew up from the beach and joined her.

''Beggar,'' she whispered when he cocked his long beak and shyly regarded her. Laughing, she held out her empty hands to the tall bird that seemed to be so awkwardly perched on his stiltlike legs.

She laughed as a flock of brown pelicans soared and dove into the bay. When Lucas climbed out of the pool, he told her that pesticides in the fifties had almost obliterated brown pelicans in south Texas, but that they were making a comeback. She forgot her joy in the birds and came up to him and wrapped a towel around his broad shoulders. With another towel she dried his hair.

When she was done, she ran her hands through the damp strands and then blushed. ''Thank you for tonight. For this week.''

He put a fingertip under her chin and guided her sweet face to his and gave her a long kiss, which held both fire and ice. Instantly he felt that intense hunger for her that ran so very deeply in him.

What he felt for her was both spiritual and physical. It was timeless. She was everything.

With her mouth she began to explore the sensitive hollow at the base of his throat. He kissed her, and as always the delicate taste of her acted upon him like an aphrodisiac.

"Let's forget supper and go inside," he said hoarsely.

Slowly she slid her hands across his wide bare chest, down the length of each of his scars.

"How did this happen?" she asked, thinking the jagged marks were scars, as everyone did.

"They are nothing. I was born with them."

"Birthmarks?" she said in a low voice. "How odd. They look more like scars."

Her gaze grew very bright, very serious when he laughed and told her about the Indian nurse who had infuriated his Christian father when she'd said his baby son had acquired the strange marks in another life, that they were marks left from scars—probably when he had died. "She said I was slashed to death by something big and heavy—maybe a machine." He paused. "My father ranted that what she said was a ridiculous, idiotic, stupid, superstitious lie. She told him that sometimes when the air is too heavy for a dying soul to rise, it enters the body of a newborn."

"Oh." Tenderly her fingers traced the white lines and came to rest instinctively upon his heart. When he tried to circle her with his arms again, she smiled and broke away.

"Not yet," she whispered. "I'm hungry."

"So am I. But for—"

"No. Please, Lucas. Let's wait."

They had supper by the pool, and afterward they pitched horseshoes, but they gave the game up quickly, deciding it wasn't the same without the boys.

The moon rose, brightening the sky. The strange bodyguard was nowhere to be seen. But Lucas had forgotten all about him when he seized Chandra and led her inside.

He threw open the glass doors to the balcony of his bedroom so they could hear the surf and smell the tangy salt air. A faint breeze stirred the sheers, causing them to fan out in eerie silver swirls. Moonlight streamed across the bed.

For a time the lovers stayed in the shadows. She edged closer, smiling, but when he reached for her, she whispered so faintly he almost didn't hear her, "No. Wait."

Raising both her hands, she began unbuttoning each tiny pearl button of her dress. She had beautiful hands, and in the moonlight, they were the color of ivory as they gracefully skimmed up and down those glimmering buttons on her bodice.

The aqua fabric parted gradually, and she eased the silky stuff over the graceful waves of her shoulders, letting it fall slowly away into a shadowy pool at her feet. She undid her black bra, and it slid to the floor with her dress.

He tried to say more but a vast silence enveloped them, and as always they spoke without words. Then her mouth was seeking his again, no longer teasing but in deadly earnest. Every muscle in his strong arms and legs flexed. Their sexes met. Teased. And clung. Suddenly he thrust, and as she launched her hips upward to meet him halfway, he knew a wild thrill that was more powerful than any he'd ever known as he sank inside her deeply.

With her thighs, she gloved him.

When she began to move, he clasped her to him, staring into her eyes for a long moment, telling her with his mind and heart that he loved her. Only when she silently communicated the same emotions did he begin to move inside her, steadily, without stopping, as she clasped him ever tighter. He grew hot, burning hot as she drew him deeper and deeper into that swirling black flame that was soft and yet an all-encompassing velvet darkness.

As he brought her to climax after climax, a corresponding firestorm built inside him.

His arms wrapped around her like steel bands.

He was burning up.

And then exploding and soaring on long hot waves of ecstasy.

Dying. And then bursting again and again every time she cried out.

He caught her to him, filling her completely as he held her tightly beneath him. Then he heaved one final time, shuddering against her, finding his own sublime release.

For a moment they were two beings alone in their own time and space, sharing a paradise of the senses. Then he mindlessly buried his lips against her silken throat and whispered her name.

"Chandra."

Lucas had fallen asleep instantly. Not she.

For a long time Chandra lay beneath Lucas's heavy body, unmoving, as utterly spent as he, even as the electrifying name he had spoken with such passionate ardor echoed inside her.

Chandra?

Yes, she *was* Chandra. An entire lifetime had come back to her. She was Chandra Moran, who had been officially christened Bethany Ann Moran.

And Lucas?

Lucas Broderick was that awful lawyer.

Why had he made her love him?

She knew why.

The warmth that had raced through her lush body moments before chilled, and she began to feel strange, not herself, and yet really herself for the first time since the accident, as painful images and traumatic emotions and memories, some of them only half-formed and poorly understood, bombarded her.

She knew the exact moment when Lucas's heavy breathing grew more regular and he fell asleep. Then, very carefully she wriggled free. Slowly she got up and, moving as soundlessly as a sleepwalker, glided into the bathroom. Numbly she showered and put on a pair of white jeans and a white embroidered blouse.

For a long moment she studied her face in the steamy mirror, as she had so many days and nights before. Only tonight the triangular face with the high cheekbones and vivid blue eyes was no longer that of a stranger.

She was Chandra Moran—heiress.

No wonder Lucas hadn't told her who she was.

Lucas Broderick was a slick, ambitious lawyer who had a reputation for playing dirty—and winning, if his defendant was rich and able to pay. More than a few of her benefactors had had bad dealings with him.

With an eye to her fortune, he had romanced her and played her for a fool.

Exactly as Stinky Brown had so many years before. Gram had wisely had Stinky investigated, and when Gram had confronted Chandra with the unsavory stories about the other rich girls Stinky had courted and then Chandra had caught him in bed with Holly, Chandra had run away from them all.

Lucas Broderick *was* her enemy. Ugly phrases echoed in the dark places in her mind.

Lucas's deep husky drawl, heard for the first time, beloved even then as she'd hidden in the foyer closet, had made hideous promises to her family.

Utterly merciless. Destroy your cousin's name and her claim—

None of them had known she had arrived at the ranch and had been eavesdropping outside the library when Lucas had sworn to her family that he would break the will and destroy her.

More memories deluged her.

She was a child again in India, holding tightly to her stern grandmother's hand as a dark-skinned man with a white turban wrapped around his head dug up the floor of a crumbling house. Again she stared in horror at the gaping eye sockets in that tiny skull, at the dusty bones and rotten fabric in the box under the ancient rotting flooring. She had wept hysterically over that poor murdered girl because she had known, somehow she had known that some physical part of her former self was buried in that shallow grave.

Chandra had lived before, but nobody in her present family had ever believed her—not even Gram. Not even when she'd led them to her grave.

Her family had brought her back to Texas more determined than ever to erase all her memories of that other life.

Next Chandra saw a rose garden and a dark-haired girl snatching the roses Chandra had painstakingly gathered from a basket. The girl was shouting and crushing them under her cowboy boots, and Chandra said, "Don't, Holly—"

Holly, her beautiful cousin who had been so jealous of her, and the way Gram and she had loved each other. In the end Holly had taken Stinky because she always had to have everything that was Chandra's.

Next Chandra was in a closet in the Moran foyer. She'd come home after an estrangement of twelve years because Gram had written her a letter, begging her forgiveness and telling her that she was going to leave her in control of the Moran fortune. But when Chandra had called Gram from Mexico, she had been told by Stinky that Gram had died suddenly and that there was no reason for her to return.

Chandra had gone home the day of the memorial service only to discover Holly and the others in the library plotting to break Gram's will. Chandra had hidden in a closet after she had heard Lucas's voice and realized he was leaving and would catch her eavesdropping if she didn't run or hide.

She remembered the dying roses in the foyer, the lonely strangeness of the house that day without Gram. But most of all she remembered the strange way Lucas's voice had held her spellbound. It had been gravelly and rough-edged and musical as he had promised her family he would break the will and spread rumors that Chandra had used payoffs and bribery in Mexico. Even though he'd been hired to ruin her, his words had lingered and resonated almost hypnotically in some sweet secret place in Chandra's soul.

Again his cruel words and phrases came to her in horrible fits and starts.

"Utterly merciless. Destroy your cousin's name and her claim."

In freeze-framed images Chandra saw him as she'd seen him from the partially opened closet door where she'd hidden that day. She had been drawn to him even though he had given off an aura of rage and arrogance.

His brilliant gray eyes had reminded her of angry smoke from a smoldering fire. His face had seemed stark and bold. Even so, fool that she was, she'd imagined she'd sensed some inner pain behind his cruel, self-serving exterior. She'd imagined herself nurturing and easing that pain.

Worst of all, she'd felt a blinding current of emotion drawing her soul to his. Even though he hadn't seen her, he'd seemed to feel it, too. He had stopped in mid-stride, his searing gaze searching every niche and darkened corner of the hall. He had called out to her, and she'd had to bite her tongue not to reply. When he'd started toward the closet, she'd desperately begun counting backward to break the connection.

Miraculously the ploy had worked.

But when he'd stalked out of the house, she'd wanted to run after him.

Because, insane though it would seem to everybody else, she'd known why that dangerous man had the mysterious power to attract her. She had known with an unfathomable certainty what no other woman in her right mind would have believed—*that she'd known him before.*

Just as she had known that he was the one person she had been searching for all *this* life without even realizing it. Every bad-boy boyfriend her family and friends had objected to, even Stinky, had been an attempt to find *him.*

Their love had been forbidden in her former life. She had been murdered because of it. And he had died horribly, too—he'd been run over by a train—when he'd been told by her sister she'd abandoned him.

Somehow she had sensed his presence in the world and had struggled to find him.

But her new family, who except for Gram had never understood her and who had always been against her, had unwittingly hired him as a tool to destroy her.

She remembered how she had stayed in that closet feeling drained and hopeless after he had gone. How she had wanted to race after him but hadn't let herself.

And then someone had opened the door.

For some reason she still couldn't see the face. But the voice that had greeted her had been familiar. "Welcome home, Bethany. I've been waiting for you. Just like I waited for Gram the day . . . she died."

Gram . . . murdered?

She had tried to run, but strong hands had seized her.

"Gotcha!"

Chandra remembered the blinding flash of the syringe, the warm, dizzying sensation of the drug flow-ing into her veins as the world went bright white and the realization struck her that she was going to die.

But—somehow—she had escaped death.

Who had opened that closet door?

What had happened next?

Who had tried to kill her?

Was it Lucas?

Why couldn't she remember?

Instead she saw a man's body wrapped in plastic.

And this time she saw the corpse's face. This time she remembered his name and shuddered.

Miguel Santos.

Her foreman in Mexico.

Poor, dear Miguel.

Next she was on a highway, barefooted and limping, her clothes covered with blood. Santos's or her own? She was holding a gun and running straight into blinding white headlights.

She remembered a horn honking right before she crumpled in the middle of the highway.

But no more memories came.

Dear God.

Had she done murder?

Trembling, more terrified than ever before, she got in bed, careful to stay as far from Lucas as possible.

Who was he? The tender lover of the past week?

Or an unscrupulous gold digger? The lawyer her family had hired to destroy her?

Gram had said she would always be a fool about men.

Chandra stared at Lucas. His dark face looked so young, so completely relaxed and guileless, like his sons' did when they slept. In no way did he appear to be the treacherous monster she told herself he must surely be.

A tear welled in the corner of her eye. Then another. Until she was sobbing helplessly.

What explanation would he give her in the morning?

He had pretended to love her so deeply, so passionately, and she felt that she could not live a single hour without his love.

And yet she would have to.

Not knowing what to fear the most—the truth or his lies—she pulled the sheets over her shivering body and lay awake in the darkness, dread and terror filling her heart. She wept and tried to make sense of her new knowledge as she waited for the dawn.

Ten

"Gotcha!" The whisper was soft, triumphant.

The next three sounds resonated like a rattlesnake's hiss.

Click. Snap. Spin.

Chandra's drowsy mind snapped awake.

One minute she'd been lying with her head cozily nestled against Lucas's shoulder, having been lulled by his body heat into sleep despite herself. Still caught in that hazy twilight zone between dream and reality, she was about to snuggle closer to him.

The next minute she felt the cold barrel of a revolver nudge her temple.

"It's loaded, bitch."

She opened her eyes and stared, too shocked to move or make a single sound.

The monster with the dead black eyes from her nightmares loomed over her.

Only he was real.

She recognized him.

He had an innocent boyish face, dark eyes and curly auburn hair.

He had opened the closet door. He had drugged her and shot Santos and tried to shoot her, too, on that lonely stretch of highway near the border.

He had found her again. Somehow, even during those weeks of amnesia, she had sensed him tracking her.

Feeling her stiffen, Lucas opened his eyes.

"Stinky?" Lucas jerked upward, registering only a shadowy hulk holding a gun to her face.

"Move, and I'll splatter her brains all over your face, counselor."

"No, Lucas. Not Stinky." Chandra's voice fell. "It's Hal."

Sweet, gentle, baby-faced Hal. The younger brother who for whatever reason couldn't make it on his own, so Stinky had felt responsible for him. Hal was the brother Stinky had sworn to take care of after a boating accident had claimed their parents' lives and left them with only each other.

"You don't look too good, Hal," she murmured, remembering for the first time that he had been badly injured when the van had crashed.

His sallow, unshaven face was haggard. The skin around his eyes was yellowish purple. An infected cut ran jaggedly down the middle of his brow. He had unhealed scratches all over his hands. He reeked of sweat.

A silent scream rose in Chandra's throat.

"You need a doctor," she said.

"Shut up. I'm not going to fall for that sympathetic crap you spout ever again. You don't care about me. You never did."

"That's not true! You were like a brother to me."

He laughed and scowled at the same time, and she realized how little he resembled the courteous young man she'd once adored.

"You shot Miguel. You tried to shoot me, too," she said. "Why?"

"Bitch! Thief! Because I was angry about the will! You walked away twelve years ago—so high and mighty—like you didn't give a damn for the old lady's money or how you hurt Stinky."

"He slept with my cousin."

"I had to stay and help him get over you. I had to take crap from your grandmother. While you—"

"I didn't have it so easy, Hal. I worked very hard."

"Well, you won't get away from me this time. Neither will you, counselor."

As Chandra stared from Hal to Lucas, she was remembering everything that had happened. Gram had sent her that first letter about the foundation in which she explained her late-in-life change of heart about what she wanted to do with her money. Apparently she'd had some sort of mystical experience at Skippy Hendrix's funeral when she'd watched a crop-duster pal of his scatter Skippy's ashes near a favorite windmill. She had decided that the money wasn't fun for the family anymore. Stinky had married Holly for it, and now everybody was just sitting around making each other miserable while they waited for the old lady to die. Gram had decided that Chandra had had the right idea all along—that the money should be given to people who really needed it. Chandra had called to talk to her grandmother, only to learn she was dead.

Chandra remembered Miguel driving her to Texas. They'd arrived too late for the memorial service, but just in time to discover her family plotting against her with their lawyer. She'd heard Lucas's voice and recognized him as her other half. Then Hal had opened that dark closet and drugged her.

Hours later she had awakened bound and gagged in a fetal position in the cellar. Then Hal had carried her out to the van and locked her inside, beside Miguel's bloody corpse. Hal had laughed when he'd told her he would burn the van with her inside. He'd said he hadn't liked sucking up to the Morans all those years and that he wasn't about to let all the Moran money go to Mexico.

More terrible than all the rest had been the claustrophobic feeling that had overwhelmed her in that darkened, locked van as her drugged brain had pondered her impending doom. That's when she had suddenly recalled how she had been murdered before.

Vividly she remembered dirt sifting through the top of a box as her own sister had buried her alive. Chandra had clawed at the boards until her fingers were raw long after her sister had left her to die, long after she'd known she had no recourse other than to surrender to that final darkness.

As Hal had started the van with murder in his heart, she had gone mad with the fierce will to destroy him. So mad that her passion had obliterated the drug's lethal power as she'd lain there and calculated a means of escape.

Groping in the darkness, she had somehow freed her bound hands and untied her feet. Then she had dug through the compartment until she found the jack. Crawling woozily over Santos's bloody body, she had crept behind Hal and slammed the jack into his head. When he'd whirled to counterattack, the speeding van had weaved crazily. She had grabbed the wheel, sideswiping a car before the van careened off an embankment and rolled.

There had been an explosion of glass and crumpling metal. When she woke up, she was lying beside Hal. The front of his forehead was split wide open. Blood was all over his face, matting his hair, drenching her clothes and his. When she had tried to help him, he had grabbed her by the hair and picked up his gun and a gasoline can.

"Gotcha," he'd whispered, right before he'd started laughing.

But as he had uncapped the gasoline can and cocked the hammer of the revolver, a fat woman from the car they'd hit had yelled at them. "Lady, do you have a car phone? My little boy's bleeding something awful."

When Hal had stared toward her distractedly, Chandra had grabbed his gun and pointed it at him.

"You haven't got the guts, Beth!" Hal had taunted, charging her.

She pulled the trigger. But her hand shook so much, she hit the van, which caught fire. When Hal rushed her, Chandra ran straight into the path of an oncoming truck.

Hal's contemptuous voice jolted her to the present.

"You won't get away this time, bitch, and neither will your lover."

"You're the one who won't get away with this," Lucas warned.

For the first time Chandra remembered Lucas. "Let him go, Hal. He doesn't really have anything to do with this."

"Oh, doesn't he? You little fool! Who do you think convinced me that we shouldn't try to talk you into a compromise about the will? Who convinced me I had to destroy your good name and kill you? Everything I did was his idea!"

"No—" Lucas broke off. "I know what you're thinking, but, Chandra—"

"Do you?" she whispered. "Do you really? I don't think so. You're a very good actor. But are you even human? I read all those articles about you, and I wouldn't let myself believe you were as cruel and predatory and greedy as everybody said you were. But now . . . You slept with me when I was sick and ill and too confused to know what I was doing. You used me. You took advantage of me. Why?"

"I love you."

"Don't lie to me now. Don't you ever lie to me again. I—I mistakenly thought I was someone special to you."

"You are."

"Well, you aren't to me." She fought to ignore the sharp glimmer of silent pain in his eyes. "Not anymore."

"Hear that, counselor?" Hal whispered. "She's got you figured for the no-good scum you are."

"Tell her the truth!" Lucas snarled.

Hal laughed. "You're damned good, counselor. I'd almost believe you if I didn't know better. Framing her was your idea. You told Stinky not to interfere with the bad publicity about her because it was good for our case."

"What publicity?" Chandra whispered.

"You're wanted for murder, sweetheart," Hal said. "Counselor Broderick here was damned smart to recognize you at the hospital and take you home and keep you all to himself, and now everybody thinks you did murder Santos 'cause you ran. Yes, sir. You've been very helpful, counselor."

"Chandra—" When Lucas reached for her, Chandra shrank away from him.

"Is that true, too, Lucas?"

"Damn it, no!" He hesitated. She continued to stare at him. "Well, not exactly. I mean—"

"Stinky *did* call you," she whispered, remembering the familiar voice she hadn't recognized until now even though it had terrified her.

Hal pulled a wadded front page from a recent newspaper out of his back pocket and pitched it to her.

Chandra straightened the crumpled newspaper and began to read. Her throat went dry. Black print began to blur. Every sentence made the hollowness inside her breast expand.

She was wanted for Miguel's murder. For a hit-and-run accident in which a woman's little boy had been badly injured.

"You shot Santos," Chandra croaked. "You were driving the van. Not me."

"But, thanks to Stinky, I have an airtight alibi. And thanks to Counselor Broderick everybody thinks it was you."

Her gaze fell to the newspaper again. There was a second article, full of vicious rumors about her. She'd heard Lucas promise to spread such rumors that day in the library. There were stories about payoffs and bribes and a corrupt system for selecting the families for which her houses would be built. An investigation into her charitable organization had been launched.

Sickened by the filth and the blatant lies, she dropped the paper without bothering to read every word. She looked at Lucas in stricken bewilderment.

"You kept me a virtual prisoner in your house while you...while you and Stinky and Hal spread these lies. You didn't want me to read newspapers or look at television because you were afraid I would learn the truth about you before you totally destroyed my good name."

"No." To Hal, he said, "Damn it. Tell her the truth."

"I already have, counselor. Everything you think is true, Beth, except that part about Stinky. He was trying to find you because he was afraid of what I might do to you if I got to you first. You see, Stinky suspected the truth about our parents' deaths. And the truth was that I murdered them. I took the plug out of their boat because they were so worried about me they were going to put me in a special school. When they got out into deep water, their boat filled and sank. I had taken the life jackets off the boat, hoping they would drown. Their bodies washed onto the beach a week later."

"That's horrible," she whispered.

"Stinky loved me anyway. See, he understood that I couldn't be locked up. He as much as told me so at their funeral. He said he'd always take care of me. And he has. I'd die for Stinky, same as he'd die for me. It was me and him—way before you or Holly ever entered the picture. He always had this knack of making himself irresistible to women. We decided that if he married a rich enough woman, there would be a living in it for the two of us. Only thing is, Stinky tends to get too involved with his women. He forgets our mission and lets them run over him. Like you did when you ran out on him twelve years ago. Like Debra before you. Like Holly now."

"Who's Debra?" she asked even though she was afraid she already knew.

"The girl Stinky was engaged to before he met you."

"The one he beat up?"

"Stinky never laid a hand on any woman."

"But—"

"Oh, he went to jail for beating her after she jilted him. Only he didn't beat her. I did. That's how come Stinky has been so all-fired determined to find you before I did. He has a way of sensing my true feelings even when I try to hide them. He went to jail for me that one time even though he was mad at me for hitting Debra. I don't want to make him mad by hurting nobody again, but I can't let you take all the money."

"Hal, if I die, the money will still go into the foundation."

"You think you're real smart, Beth. You think I don't know that?" Hal pulled the hammer back. "At least you won't get to be the one to enjoy it."

Some strange new element, a total finality, in his hard voice and eyes made her more afraid.

"Chandra, be quiet," Lucas warned. "He's gone completely crazy."

"I'm not crazy!" With an evil smile he shifted the gun to Lucas.

Even though Hal was shaking violently and his finger was on the trigger, Chandra never really thought he'd do it.

The sudden blast was loud and obscene.

There was a blaze of fire, and Lucas fell back against the pillows, a black hole gaping in his brown shoulder, a stain of red seeping from beneath his body.

With a cry, Chandra knelt over him, her eyes glazed and tearful.

Hal yanked her away by the hair.

"Forget him!"

"But—"

His fist slammed into her jaw.

Someone was stuffing something that tasted of sour sweat and dust into her mouth, and she was strangling on the wretchedly thick cloth.

As Chandra tried to turn her head she realized she was lying on hard, clammy concrete in some dank, dark place that smelled of mildew and mold. Her hands were bound so tightly behind her, the muscles in her arms were cramping.

But it wasn't her discomfort that brought her sharply to consciousness. It was Lucas's low-pitched whisper near her ear.

"Chandra."

She opened her eyes.

Lucas's dear, white, strained face hovered inches over hers. At first she thought she was dreaming. Then she saw the blood all over his chest.

He was alive.

He finished gagging her and eased her head gently against the concrete.

"Nice work, counselor. As always."

Lucas's gray eyes were cold and dark and utterly soulless as he slowly got up.

Hal giggled. "May you rest in peace, dear Bethany." He turned off the light.

And Chandra realized she was in the tunnel under the house that would be permanently sealed with concrete tomorrow.

And Lucas was walking away.

With Hal.

They were going to bury her alive.

Something small and awful with lots of disgusting legs scuttled across her lips. She tried to scream, but the gag choked off all sound.

Dear God.

Suddenly the darkness was a living thing, a suffocating force pressing down upon her. She began to writhe and twist so hard and fast that soon she couldn't breathe.

She lay back, exhausted, her heart hammering, as she forced herself to take slow, measured breaths.

Lucas was one of them.

She had dreamed it. She had known it all along.

Only she hadn't wanted to believe it.

Until now.

Nameless, paralyzing horror swelled inside her when she heard Hal chuckle again. Then he shut the big door with a ringing clang that echoed endlessly in that hollow chasm.

But the silence afterward was far more chilling.

Eleven

———

Lucas stumbled out of the garage.

The breeze had died to a whisper. The night sky was steamy purple and so hotly aglow it seemed to burn with a fever.

Or was it just Lucas who was burning up because a bullet had passed through him? Because he had helped lock Chandra in a hellish place that terrified her?

"Move it, counselor. You may be half dead already, but I want to do you over by the pool."

The searing pain in his right shoulder blocked all feeling in his other nerves. Lucas couldn't feel his legs as he moved slowly forward, holding the blood-soaked towel against the bullet wound to staunch the flow. He walked with the listless gait of a zombie. Maybe it was the loss of blood that made him feel so numb, but he didn't think so.

What had really gotten him was the look of utter despair in Chandra's eyes when she'd become convinced that he was a brute and a killer.

"Get down on your knees, counselor. I'll let you say a prayer before you die."

Lucas's eyes narrowed. His heart convulsed with hate.

"I'm gonna do you like that crazy serial killer said he would, so everybody will think he shot you. Then I'll wait up for your kids and do them, too."

The boys.

Fresh hatred flooded Lucas. All his fear was gone. He had to save Chandra. He would die or he would kill.

"I said kneel, counselor."

Lucas sagged weakly beside a wrought-iron lawn chair.

"Put your head down on the ground and your hands on the back of your head."

Lucas felt his life slow to a beat as he lowered his head to the damp grass. Another beat.

He was going to die.

If he didn't do something fast.

Now.

But even before his left hand closed like a vise around the leg of the lawn chair and he slung the heavy piece of furniture straight at Hal, Hal had screamed in pain. The gun jumped a fraction of a second before it went off, causing the bullet to plow into the grass an inch away from Lucas's face.

The bastard was rubbing his hand and moaning in pain. He had missed.

The revolver and a horseshoe clattered onto the concrete apron by the pool.

Peppin had flung the horseshoe with deadly precision. He raced forward and kicked the gun and horseshoe into the pool.

Hal was lunging for the gun like a madman when Lucas tackled him and hurled him hard against the concrete.

Hal's skull cracked. Too stunned to move for a second or two, he just lay there. When he finally opened his eyes, Lucas attacked him like a demon, his balled fists pounding his jaw and stomach relentlessly.

Both boys dived into the pool for the gun.

Peppin burst to the surface with the gun and Montague with the horseshoe. Lucas had his hands around Hal's throat and was squeezing the life out of him.

"Go ahead. Kill him, Dad!"

"Yeah! Go for it!"

Peppin's and Montague's blood lust and cheering penetrated Lucas's crazed brain, and he suddenly realized that the large brown hands on that thick throat were his own.

In a daze Lucas jerked them away and stared at the unconscious Hal like a man awakening from a dream.

Then Montague said, "Dad, you're bleeding."

"He shot me."

Then Peppin asked, "Where's Chandra?"

Oh, God. "The tunnel!" Lucas whispered.

She was lying as still and rigid as a corpse when she heard the first muffled sounds.

Then the door banged open, and she heard Peppin and Montague fighting over who got to go in first.

Lucas's deep, husky voice boomed inside the tunnel.

"Chandra, we've come back!"

The light was turned on.

"I get to untie her."

"No, I do."

"I threw the horseshoe."

"Metal mouth! Stupid!"

"Nerd!"

And the boys were there, hovering over her, squabbling exactly as they had when she'd regained consciousness in their closet.

They loosened her gag and eased it away from her mouth.

"My two darling angels."

The boys beamed.

She hugged them and tried to smile. But she wept instead.

When Lucas hesitantly knelt beside her, her beautiful face whitened and became filled with distress. She flinched and began to tremble. "Please! Please! Don't let him touch me!"

"But I love you," Lucas whispered, frantic to make her understand. "I would never hurt you. Never."

"Liar," she whispered, clutching the boys. "You already have." She began to weep again. "Get him away from me!" That was the last thing he heard, because he fainted.

Nobody believed her.

Not the boys.

Not the police.

Even after she was out of the tunnel, Chandra was still scared.

Within minutes after Peppin called the police, Lucas's house was part madhouse, part war zone. Ambulances and police cars littered his driveway, their colored lights twisting and blinking as the boys raced excitedly from one cop to the next, bragging more each time they retold the night's adventure.

Chandra and Lucas and the two bodyguards and Hal were all lying on gurneys, about to be put in separate ambulances. The boys, with Lucas's and Chandra's help, were trying to explain everything.

A surge of fear flowed through Chandra every time Lucas came near her or tried again to tell her he loved her. She would beg the police to keep him away from her.

"No," she kept saying to him, forcing herself to ignore the silent agony in his eyes. "Stay away from me." And to anyone in a uniform who would listen, she said, "Why won't you believe me? I tell you, he was one of them."

Twelve

———

Lucas's firm occupied the top two floors of a downtown office building and commanded the city's finest views of the sparkling bay. Despite the oppressive heat, the office felt as crisply cool as an alpine summer day.

Usually the elegant suite was as quiet as a bank vault or a hallowed sanctuary. Usually legal aids and lawyers and their clients spoke between these marble walls in the same hushed, reverent voices they might use at a funeral.

Not today.

Excited adolescent shouts from the aluminum-walled elevator could be heard even before the chrome doors burst open and the Broderick boys exploded into the huge reception area like a matched pair of rowdy volcanoes, each zooming straight for Lucas's office.

Not that Lucas's legal secretary, who knew how cranky Lucas had been of late, didn't try to halt them.

"You can't go in there!" she snapped primly in that no-nonsense tone most people wisely obeyed. "He's with a—"

They brushed past her and kicked his door open. Lucas's dark face looked thin and worn as his head snapped up. Not that he hadn't heard them coming.

He still felt a little weak. He hadn't fully recovered from the bullet wound.

His silver eyes narrowed explosively.

"Dad!" Peppin waved a torn piece of paper like a tattered banner. "Chandra finally wrote to us. She invited us to Mexico."

"That's nice," Lucas said in a dull, lost tone. "I'm very happy for you. She won't give me the time of day."

"You've gotta quit being so sulky and stubborn just because she sent a few of your old letters back."

"Me—sulky and stubborn? She sent *all* my letters back! And all my flowers! She won't take my calls! She had me stopped at the border and arrested when I tried— I spent a night in jail with half a dozen drunks. Do you remember that? Do you? A guy punched me. And I started hemorrhaging again."

No woman, not even Joan, had ever made him feel so low. So unwanted. So abandoned. So utterly bereft and alone.

"You've gotta go down there again and be nice and bring her back. We'll help you," Peppin said.

A big leather chair swiveled. Then a man's sharp boom of laughter from the depths of the chair made both boys jump. "Chandra had you thrown into jail? Why the hell didn't you tell me?"

For the first time the boys grew aware of the dangerous and powerful-looking man with the jet black hair seated in the big leather chair in front of their father's desk.

"Don't tell anybody. I'm not especially proud of that night," Lucas grumbled. "It would be the last straw with my partners."

The boys stood stock-still and went mute as they registered the charismatic stranger's presence.

"Hello, guys," the man said, eyeing them, and then Lucas, expectantly.

"Boys, this is Mr. Rafe Steele." Lucas introduced everybody grumpily.

Peppin let out a war whoop.

Montague whispered in awe, "Chandra's friend! You're the bodyguard. Do you really know Jo Jo and his heavy metal band?"

Rafe nodded and flashed them a warm smile. "I was his personal bodyguard till I got smart and walked off the job. He's a jerk. Hey—but it sounds like the three of you were accidental bodyguards...for Chandra. I owe you."

"We love her. We've gotta get her back, Mr. Steele. Will you help us?"

"Funny, I was just telling your father the same thing. But he wouldn't listen, even though I can vouch for the fact that this past month Chandra's been miserable without the three of you."

The boys rushed closer, no longer afraid of the big, tough-looking stranger in their father's chair.

"Dad, you've gotta let Rafe do something. And fast. Before we lose her forever."

"No! And that's final! Consider her lost. She left." He hesitated. "Look, I don't like it any better than you do, but she's made up her mind. I was a bastard to her. And she hates me."

But Rafe countered, "No, she doesn't. She's made peace with her family—even Holly. If she can forgive them and compromise with them, she can damn sure forgive you."

"I said no." Lucas's low voice was lethal.

"What if I told you she was pregnant?"

Lucas's gray eyes lit up as if a match had been struck.

Watching those eyes blaze and his face whiten as the news sank in, the boys smiled at each other and then slapped their right hands together.

Lucas's lips thinned at their burst of unwelcome applause, but he neither lashed out at them nor objected when Rafe said, "Hear me out, guys. I have a plan."

Chandra hadn't found a suitable replacement for her driver, dear, sweet, Miguel Santos, and never had she missed anybody more than she missed him. She had some sort of stomach virus, which lowered her energy level to zero, and she was doing his job and hers, as well.

Which was good, in a way. Because she was too tired and too overworked and too ill to think or to mourn—

No. She wouldn't let herself think of them.

For an instant she saw Lucas's fierce beloved dark face. She saw his gray eyes, which had been glazed with pain in the hospital when she'd told him good-bye. He had looked so downcast. So utterly rejected, with his chest bandaged and his right arm in a sling.

No. She wouldn't let herself think of him. Because the agony of that loss and betrayal was still so keen and raw it scared her.

Sweat streamed from under Chandra's Stetson as she turned the steering wheel of the huge truck, which was heavily loaded with roof panels. She shifted, panting as she ground the gears inexpertly, and the heavy vehicle clumsily weaved into the barrio where two of her church groups had houses under construction.

Hal was being held in jail without bond. He had confessed to planting drugs in her van and then later in one of her houses. He had stolen her bloody T-shirt from the hospital and mailed it to the police. Stinky had admitted that he had lied when he'd said Hal had been with them the night of the wreck. The government had halted its investigation of her operation. She had been completely exonerated, and all her backers had regained their confidence in her. And the serial killer who had threatened Lucas had been caught and was behind bars, as well.

Even so, ever since she'd returned to Mexico, she'd had too much to do. She was depressed and stressed to the max.

For one thing, it was hot. A sweltering one hundred and fifteen degrees in the scant shade of a mes-quite tree, to be exact. Today the cab felt like an oven.

Maybe that was the reason for the trouble at site four.

Rafe had said that three of the volunteers were real troublemakers.

Which was odd. Usually people who signed on to help with their church group were willing to endure great physical hardship for the single week it took to build a house. Trouble-prone teenagers often worked even harder than their adult chaperones. Rafe and Cathy had said they were at their wits' end with this particular trio, and they'd asked her to personally drop by and try to say a few words to inspire them.

The barrio street was unpaved and deeply rutted, and brown dust churned from behind the truck's big black wheels. Dozens of small children in dirty, ragged clothes raced from their hovels into the street, braving the dust and the flies to grin brightly and wave at her, for she was a much-beloved figure in this neighborhood. She smiled and waved back. But not for long. With only one hand on the wheel, the truck lurched sharply to the right, rattling violently and nearly hitting a cactus plant.

The truck didn't have power steering, and since the seat couldn't be moved, she could barely reach the worn clutch pedal even when she sat as far forward as possible. So it took all her strength and all her concentration just to drive.

Except for the summer heat and the constant oppression of poverty, worse now because of the long drought and recent political corruption in Mexico City, Piedras Negras was a nice town—as Mexican border towns go. Flat, pale ranchland, parched bone-white by the drought, and the sluggish brown Rio

Grande girded the city. But the blue sky was roomy, and the desolate location made for less prostitution and crime, so the town seemed more like the rural towns in the interior.

Thick dust coated the vine growing on the barbed wire fence surrounding the building site. The walls of site three were ten feet high, which was why Chandra was bringing that group roof panels.

She frowned when she saw site four, where the walls had only two layers of concrete blocks, and they seemed to already be slanting inward.

Oh, dear.

This was trouble.

If the church group didn't finish by Saturday, and there was no way they could short of a miracle, Chandra would fall behind schedule and build one less house. Which meant one of the deserving families in the barrio who had won her lottery would not have a house until next year.

Chandra pulled the emergency brake up, then banged on her door and cried out to the job foreman that she needed a strong man to open the door or she couldn't get out. She'd bought the truck used. It was so old and battered the doors could only be opened from the outside, and only by a very husky individual.

When two men who had been laying a third row of cinder blocks set their forty-pound blocks down and rushed toward her, the foreman grabbed them by their shoulders and ordered them to keep working.

Chandra felt confusion and irritation.

Until the foreman sent a skinny, familiar-looking boy who had been mixing thick white mortar in a tub over to the far corner of the building site. With dawning horror she watched the lanky messenger pull off his surgical mask and lean over a tall man who was reclining as lazily as a Spanish conquistador in the hammock.

The tall man's face was covered by a cowboy hat, his lean, line-backer's frame stretched full length under the shade of a fluttering tarp. Chandra couldn't help but feel disgust when she noted the dozen or so church women with their sunburned cheeks and noses slaving under the blazing mid-morning sun.

The man shot up, his gray eyes instantly piercingly alert as he tipped his wide-brimmed hat toward her. When he recognized her, he grinned in startled surprise and pleasure. He shot upright. Then his long strides carried him swiftly toward Chandra.

Lucas.

The lanky messenger was Montague.

"No!"

Rafe had tricked her. She lunged at the door to escape.

But it wouldn't budge.

She was trapped.

Until somebody released her.

"Somebody—let me out!" she screamed frantically, searching for her site foreman, who had mysteriously disappeared. As had most of the other workers.

Lucas opened the truck door, and she practically fell into his arms.

Her hands grabbed at him for support, one hand closing around his denim-clad thigh, the other his waist. Clumsily she levered herself up his body.

"Hey, that was kind of fun," he whispered, so jauntily she longed to slap him. Of course she couldn't do that. Not in front of the big-eyed church women.

"Well, what are you looking at?" she yelled at the women.

"Hey, don't get so riled," Lucas whispered. "It's not their fault."

"No! It's yours! I hate you!"

"Are you sure about that?" He clasped her tighter.

He was hot, and so was she. But he felt good, so incredibly good, so good she felt another touch of vertigo. Suddenly she was breathless.

For four long, agonizing weeks she had slept alone and tried to forget him.

She was still sure she could, in time, so she pushed frantically at his chest. But it was like trying to budge a steel wall with her puny strength.

"I love you," he whispered, pressing her closer. "I love you."

"No."

"Forgive me," he begged hoarsely, his low voice so strangely choked she thought he might be about to cry.

The broken sound caught at her heart, and she couldn't resist glancing at him.

Their eyes locked. His rugged face was fierce. He wasn't weeping, but the all-powerful emotion she read in his eyes was more profound than tears.

I love you. Believe me. Because I'll die if you don't. I forgive you.

It took them a moment to realize that neither of them had spoken. At least not with words.

And yet they had.

In their own special way.

Then his face softened, and he enfolded her in a crushing embrace.

She couldn't fight him any more than she could fight herself. All her life she had been looking for him. At last she had found him. And she knew that no matter what he had done, no matter who he was, she wanted to be with him always.

Quiet tears of joy slid down her cheeks. "Thank you for coming," she whispered. "I was such a fool. Of course, I forgive you. For that is the nature and power of true love."

"I tried to come before. I spent a night cooling my heels in one sorry Mexican jail cell with some pretty disgusting individuals."

"I know. I'm sorry."

Chandra clung to him, aware of a thrilling happiness as she surrendered her lips to his hard mouth in giddy delirium.

As he kissed her, only vaguely was she aware of two hands slapping each other triumphantly in the background, of two excited adolescent voices that were belovedly familiar.

"So, is she or isn't she going to have a baby sister?"

"Or a baby brother."

"When's he gonna ask her and give her the ring?"

"Shh! Let 'im kiss her first, stupid."

"Not stupid."

"At times you are. Girls like kisses."

"Boys, too."

"Just sissies."

Slowly the quick, pulsating phrases and words became recognizable as the voices of her darling boys. Her angels.

Her sons.

They wanted to know if she was going to have a baby sister.

A baby?

The thought electrified her.

Never once had she considered that wonderful possibility. She had just thought her stomach was upset from nerves or from something in the border food. She remembered how oddly Rafe had looked at her every time she had insisted that was all it was, how solicitous he'd been, how determined he'd been in his search for a new driver.

Rafe was a father himself. He must know the signs.

Her mind raced backward. She always felt sickest in the morning. Suddenly she was nearly positive that she was, indeed, going to have Lucas's baby. How could she have been so blind?

"Marry me," Lucas said when at last he withdrew his lips.

"Yes. Oh, yes. Yes. Yes," she whispered, right before she reached up and kissed him again.

A long time later she thought she heard two hands come together in another loud slap.

"See, I told you, stupid."

"Not stupid!"

It was she who had been stupid. She who had carelessly thrown away the three people in the whole world she cared most about.

She would have to spend the rest of her life making it up to them.

The breathless kiss she gave Lucas was only the beginning.

Epilogue

Below their charming hotel, Posada la Ermita, which was perched loftily on a hill, the colonial Mexican town with its cobblestone streets, jacaranda trees and many churches dozed quietly in the hazy, pink and lavender light.

"I told you San Miguel de Allende was the perfect place for our honeymoon," Chandra said to Lucas as she came out onto the tiled balcony of their suite just as a white-coated waiter arrived to set the table so they could enjoy a private dinner with the boys after they finished swimming.

The air was refreshingly crisp and cool after the summer heat of Texas. The sound of water splashing in the nearby fountain and the plaintive notes of a Spanish guitar in a cantina could be heard.

Lucas set his beer down and got up to help her to a chair.

Her face was glowing in the rosy sunlight. The last rays burnished her golden hair, making it look like flame. Her blue eyes were radiant. He had paid the boys a fortune to stay away all day and had spent the afternoon making love to her while the boys had explored the village and cavorted down at the pool.

"Aren't the views and the sunlight wonderful?" she asked, staring at the lime green jacaranda trees and a trellis brimming with purple bougainvillea.

"Wonderful," he agreed, squeezing her hand, but he was looking at her.

"That's why it's been an artist colony for years," she continued. "Except for the church bells, it's very quiet."

There were dozens of bell towers, and the bells started ringing before dawn and didn't stop until well after midnight.

"It's damned hard for the ordinary tourist to get to."

They had come in a friend's private plane.

"You're spoiled, my love," she said.

Furious shouts drifted up from the pool. The boys, who had been told to watch for the waiter and their dinner and to come up as soon as they saw him, had forgotten that parental order and were fighting over a pair of flippers and a float.

Lucas smiled at her. "The boys are as noisy as the church bells."

"I don't mind their noise," she whispered.

"I guess you'd better get used to it, since we're well on our way to a house full of kids."

The waiter left them.

"Oh, Chandra," Lucas said, pulling her close and burying his face in her golden hair. "All this happiness is going to take some getting used to."

She clung to him just as tightly. "I feel the same way. I still can't believe—"

"What?"

"That I finally found you."

"That again?"

"I know you don't believe in reincarnation—"

"That's right. One lifetime of happiness is definitely all I would ever ask for," he stared, kissing her so she couldn't reply.

Dinner was over.

"So, Dad, if those birthmarks on your chest were really scars and you two knew each other in another life, were we there, too?" Peppin asked his father.

"Look, one lifetime is enough of a challenge for me," Lucas said. "Like I keep saying, I'm not at all sure I can buy into this reincarnation theory. I don't remember anything about any other life in India."

"That's 'cause you weren't murdered, Dad!" Montague inserted in a sage tone.

"What does being murdered have to do with anything?"

"Just everything! I'll loan you my favorite book, *Psychic Vampires,* and then you'll understand. Murdered people are more likely to remember their past lives."

"Thanks. But I'll pass." Lucas chuckled. "Loving Chandra now, in this lifetime, on this side of the world, is miracle enough for me."

* * *

Chandra was standing naked in the mists of their hotel bedroom's shower when Lucas stepped in and joined her.

Their eyes met.

As they had before.

Without speaking, she picked up the bar of soap and began running it over his thighs and abdomen in electrifying circles that made his brown skin heat.

He grabbed her wrist and shoved her gently against the wall. The bar of soap fell and slid to the drain. Lucas stepped over it.

In a wild outpouring of sexual exultation, he picked up his wife and fitted her snugly against his hips, driving inside her.

Their sexes joined, their souls, as well. She wrapped her legs around him and let her swanlike neck fall back as gracefully as a ballerina so that warm water streamed over her face and hair and swirled around their naked forms.

She had never felt so hot or so good. As if he and she were made of some molten liquid that flowed together and became one.

Without realizing it, he began to move.

She said his name, over and over, and her low, soft, staccato voice made it so incredibly erotic he came.

She exploded, too.

For a long time he clasped her hips to his, wanting to stay inside her forever.

It had never been this sublime with anyone. It never would.

What he felt for her was beyond love. Beyond time.

Beyond this world and all eternity.

He picked her up and carried her to the bed, where he patted her naked body dry with a towel.

She crawled on top of him, and kissed the new bullet wound. With her tongue she traced the long white birthmarks that crisscrossed his torso.

She looked into his eyes and smiled that dazzling smile that he felt he had always known.

And he wondered. In spite of himself, he wondered.

And he knew he always would.

* * * * *

SILHOUETTE® *Desire*®

COMING NEXT MONTH

#1009 THE COWBOY AND THE KID—Anne McAllister
July's *Man of the Month*, rodeo cowboy Taggart Jones, vowed never to remarry, but his little girl had other plans for him—and every one involved feisty schoolmarm Felicity Albright.

#1010 A GIFT FOR BABY—Raye Morgan
The Baby Shower
All Hailey Kingston wanted was to go to her friend's baby shower. Instead, she was stuck on a remote ranch, with a handsome cowboy as her keeper. But the longer she stayed in Mitch Harper's arms, the less she wanted to leave!

#1011 THE BABY NOTION—Dixie Browning
Daddy Knows Last
Priscilla Barrington wanted a baby, so she planned a visit to the town sperm bank. But then she met Jake Spencer! Could she convince the rugged cowboy to father her child—the old-fashioned way?

#1012 THE BRIDE WORE BLUE—Cindy Gerard
Northern Lights Brides
When Maggie Adams returned home, she never expected to see her childhood neighbor Blue Hazzard. Could the former gawky teenager turned hunk teach Maggie how to love again?

#1013 GAVIN'S CHILD—Caroline Cross
Bachelors and Babies
Gavin Cantrell was stunned to return home and learn that his estranged wife Annie had given birth to his child without telling him. Now that he was back, would his dream of being a family man be fulfilled?

#1014 MONTANA FEVER—Jackie Merritt
Made in Montana
Independent Lola Fanon never met anyone as infuriating—or as irresistible—as Duke Sheridan. She knew he wasn't her type, but staying away from the handsome rancher was becoming a losing battle....

The wedding celebration was so nice...
too bad the bride wasn't there!

Runaway Brides

Find out what happens when three brides have a
change of heart.

Three complete stories by some of your favorite
authors—all in one special collection!

YESTERDAY ONCE MORE
by Debbie Macomber

FULL CIRCLE
by Paula Detmer Riggs

THAT'S WHAT FRIENDS ARE FOR
by Annette Broadrick

Available this June wherever books are sold.

Look us up on-line at:http://www.romance.net

Silhouette®
™

SREQ696

This July, watch for the delivery of...

An exciting new miniseries that appears in a different Silhouette series each month. It's about love, marriage—and Daddy's unexpected need for a baby carriage!

Daddy Knows Last unites five of your favorite authors as they weave five connected stories about baby fever in New Hope, Texas.

- **THE BABY NOTION** by Dixie Browning
  (SD#1011, 7/96)

- **BABY IN A BASKET** by Helen R. Myers
  (SR#1169, 8/96)

- **MARRIED...WITH TWINS!**
  by Jennifer Mikels
  (SSE#1054, 9/96)

- **HOW TO HOOK A HUSBAND (AND A BABY)**
  by Carolyn Zane
  (YT#29, 10/96)

- **DISCOVERED: DADDY** by Marilyn Pappano
  (IM#746, 11/96)

Daddy Knows Last arrives in July...only from

SILHOUETTE DESIRE® "CELEBRATION 1000" SWEEPSTAKES
OFFICIAL RULES—NO PURCHASE NECESSARY

To enter, complete an Official Entry Form or a 3"x5" card by hand printing "Silhouette Desire Celebration 1000 Sweepstakes," your name and address, and mail it to: In the U.S.: Silhouette Desire Celebration 1000 Sweepstakes, P.O. Box 9069, Buffalo, NY 14269-9069, or In Canada: Silhouette Desire Celebration 1000 Sweepstakes, P.O. Box 637, Fort Erie, Ontario L2A 5X3. Limit one entry per envelope. Entries must be sent via first-class mail and be received no later than 6/30/96. No liability is assumed for lost, late or misdirected mail.

Prizes: Grand Prize—an original painting (approximate value $1500 U.S.);300 Runner-up Prizes—an autographed Silhouette Desire® Book (approximate value $3.50 U.S./$3.99 CAN. each). Winners will be selected in a random drawing (to be conducted no later than 9/30/96) from among all eligible entries received by D.L. Blair, Inc., an independent judging organization whose decision is final.

Sweepstakes offer is open only to residents of the U.S. (except Puerto Rico) and Canada who are 18 years of age or older, except employees and immediate family members of Harlequin Enterprises Ltd., their affiliates, subsidiaries, and all agencies, entities and persons connected with the use, marketing or conduct of this sweepstakes. All federal, state, provincial, municipal and local laws apply. Offer void where prohibited by law. Taxes and/or duties are the sole responsibility of the winners. Any litigation within the province of Quebec respecting the conduct and awarding of prizes may be submitted to the Regie des alcools des courses et des jeux. All prizes will be awarded; winners will be notified by mail. No substitution for prizes is permitted. Odds of winning are dependent upon the number of eligible entries received.

Grand Prize winner must sign and return an Affidavit of Eligibility within 30 days of notification. In the event of noncompliance within this time period, prize may be awarded to an alternate winner. Any prize or prize notification returned as undeliverable may result in the awarding of that prize to an alternate winner. By acceptance of their prize, winners consent to the use of their names, photographs or likenesses for purposes of advertising, trade and promotion on behalf of Harlequin Enterprises Ltd., without further compensation unless prohibited by law. In order to win a prize, residents of Canada will be required to correctly answer a time-limited arithmetical skill-testing question administered by mail.

For a list of winners (available after October 31, 1996) send a separate self-addressed stamped envelope to: Silhouette Desire Celebration 1000 Sweepstakes Winners, P.O. Box 4200, Blair, NE 68009-4200.

SILHOUETTE®

Desire®

CELEBRATION 1000

A treasured piece of romance could be yours!

During April, May and June as part of
Desire's Celebration 1000 you can enter to win an
original piece of art used on an actual Desire cover!

Or you could win one of 300 autographed Man of the
Month books!

See Official Sweepstakes Rules for more details.

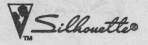